The Man Who Killed His Wife

(and What Happened Afterwards)

WOL-VRIEY

Burning Bulb
PUBLISHING

Other Books By Wol-vriey:
The Bizarro Story of I
Meat Suitcase
Chainsaw Cop Corpse
Vegan Zombie Apocalypse
Boston Posh (Bud Malone #1)
Vegan Vampire Vaginas
Vagina Mundi
Melanie Nemesis Catchpole
Bizarro 101: A Basic Primer
Boston Corpse (Bud Malone #2)
Dr. Orgasm
Boston Lust (Bud Malone #3)
Pussy Transmission
Hell Dancer
Girls Are Not Smiling
Brainchew
Brainchew 2: Out of Their Heads
Blue Nightmares
Daria (An Erotic Nightmare)
Wet Bones
Mr. Ugly
Brutal
Evil
666
The Cleaverman
Perverse
The Virgin
The Book of Atrocities
The Final Girl
Women
Ratio of Brookes to Ashleys
Delicious Zombie
Motel Gothic
The Bachelor
Marriage

Novellas and Short Stories By Wol-vriey
Big Trouble in Little Ass
Forever Ago Sunshine

The Man Who Killed His Wife
(and What Happened Afterwards)

WOL-VRIEY

Burning Bulb
PUBLISHING

The Man Who Killed His Wife
(and What Happened Afterwards)
By **Wol-vriey**

Burning Bulb Publishing
P.O. Box 4721
Bridgeport, WV 26330-4721
United States of America
www.BurningBulbPublishing.com

Cover by Melissa St. Giles.

First Edition.

Paperback Edition ISBN: 978-1-948278-69-0

CHAPTER 1

The Touchpad Court condominium stood at the west end of Raynham's Carver Street.

The three-story condominium had originally been a place of business belonging to a Mr. James Smith. But after Mr. Smith's death five years ago, the building had passed into his daughter Jennifer's hands.

(The building's 'Touchpad' name came from its late owner's business having dealt in computers and computer accessories.)

Jennifer Haskins (née Smith) was a woman who was more into esoteric religions than business, and so she'd had the place remodeled into six condo units and then sold off the lower four units, keeping one of the topmost pair of residences for she and her husband Chris, and the other for their daughter Ashley.

As a carryover from its days as a place of business, the condo had a large parking lot. It also had a nice arrangement of large trees surrounding it. But then, this was Raynham, Massachusetts. Raynham was full of trees.

All in all, the Touchpad condominium was a nice place to live in; peaceful and quiet, and yet not too far from either the Walmart Supercenter just down Broadway, or the 495 Interstate if one needed to get out of town.

Yes, the Touchpad condominium was peaceful. Its only problem was that some of its residents had very turbulent emotions.

And those turbulent emotions are what this story is all about.

CHAPTER 2

As she climbed the stairs to the third floor of the Touchpad Court condominium building that Tuesday afternoon, Maryanne Wilson tried to get a proper grip on her emotions.

Yes, I'm happily married, she told herself. *I love Bob and he loves me too. Our marriage would be perfect, if not for this small issue . . .*

Maryanne had just reached the third-floor landing and so put her thoughts on hold as she looked left, right, and center. Directly on her left was the door to the elevator, which Maryanne really only used when bringing groceries home.

The door on her far right was Ashley Haskins's condo. Maryanne could hear the loud dance music echoing from behind it. Like herself, Ashley worked from home, so there was nothing odd about her being in on a weekday afternoon.

The stairs continued on up to the roof, but Maryanne had reached her destination. Turning left, she walked along the corridor and knocked on Jennifer Haskins's door.

Jennifer opened the door and smiled at Maryanne. "Cool day, ain't it?" Then she stepped away from the door. "Come in, you're just in time for some hot coffee."

Jennifer Haskins was a slim middle-aged brunette, who this afternoon was dressed in a sweater and old jeans. As Maryanne followed her through the condo's living room into her kitchen, she wondered if she'd be able to maintain her figure as well as Maryanne had after childbirth. Jennifer had two children: Ashley and her younger brother, Chris Jnr., who now lived down in New Mexico with his family.

The two women sat in the kitchen and Jennifer poured out their mugs of coffee.

The Haskins's kitchen was on the west side of their condo unit, and from where they sat Maryanne could see the Oak Hill Mobile Home Park in the neighboring town of Taunton.

Not the best scenery, to be sure, but as Jennifer often pointed out, the profusion of trees in between somewhat compensated.

Maryanne sipped her coffee and wondered how to explain what she wanted to talk to her hostess about.

It's embarrassing to discuss, and besides, I've no idea if Jennifer can even help me out with this.

So instead, figuring that Jennifer would sooner or later steer their conversation in a direction that would naturally allow her to explain what she wanted from her, Maryanne just conversed on mundane things:

"How's Chris doing today?" she asked.

Jennifer sighed. "Still the same. The doctors say he'll improve soon, but . . . I dunno."

Chris Haskins had suffered a stroke a few months back and was now confined to a wheelchair.

"I didn't see him when I came in," Maryanne said. "Hope he's okay?"

Jennifer waved a hand towards the hallway. "He's in the bedroom."

Their coffee had both an unfamiliar tang and odor to it, clear evidence that Jennifer had once again mixed some of her weird herbs into it. The herbal ingredients themselves were open secrets, pinches taken from curiously labeled bags and jars in the kitchen cabinets and on its shelves; and not all of which were labeled in English.

Today, however, Maryanne did not bother to ask her older friend which herbs these were. Usually both women had fun discussing the holistic merits of each herb in their drinks.

But this afternoon Maryanne had other things on her mind. Once Jennifer had replied her about Chris's health, Maryanne made a non-committal gesture by way of reply. She really didn't know what more to say. She suddenly felt at a loss for how to continue the conversation.

"I really don't get it," Jennifer added after a sip of coffee. "In addition to the stuff the doctors give him, I'm giving him daily infusions of herbs that should boost his recovery, and yet it seems slower than ever."

This discussion, on the seeming slowness of Chris Haskins's recuperation from his stroke, was a common conversation topic between them.

Maryanne had more than once made the point that the slowness of Chris's recovery might well have to do with all the witch's potions that Jennifer kept feeding him, a point of view that her older friend always rejected, explaining that in her younger years she had prepared similar brews for her ailing father, which had successfully kept him alive for close to twenty years.

Maryanne, who hadn't known Jennifer that long, could not dispute this statement. But still, Maryanne felt that at the very least, Jennifer should take into consideration the fact that medications for treating stroke survivors must have changed drastically over the past twenty years; and that today's pills might not be interacting well with her holistic additions.

Whatever was the case, Chris was not recovering as fast as expected. And as far as Maryanne knew, Jennifer hadn't told her husband's doctors what she was adding to their prescriptions, or even hinted that she was doing so at all.

But there's little I can do, Maryanne thought. *The old guy isn't my husband or my responsibility. Jennifer's two children don't seem bothered about the situation. In fact, I've never once heard Ashley, who lives right next door to her mother, ever complain about the current state of her father's health.*

Maryanne hung on that last thought for a bit. *But then Ashley herself is a kettle of odd fish; so maybe in her case an abnormal reaction should be considered normal.*

"Oh, I'm sure that in time he'll show some positive improvement," Maryanne said. Then, because Jennifer looked about to burst into tears after she'd said this, she quickly reached across the kitchen table and squeezed her friend's arm. "Just hang in there; it'll work out for sure," she added. "I'm sure Chris will be back on his feet again in no time."

But for heaven's sake, lady, please stop feeding him all those creepy herbal brews, she added mentally.

"Thanks." Jennifer recovered from her threatened emotional outpouring. "Hey, you sounded bothered on the phone before you came up here. Is everything okay with you and Bob?"

Maryanne sighed loudly. Well, here it was: time to spill her guts to her friend.

"Not really," she admitted.

Jennifer's expression turned concerned. "Oh, I didn't realize that. Are you and Bob having problems?"

Now Maryanne smiled. She found it hard not to do so. "Yeah . . . you could put it like that," she began slowly. "But we're not fighting or anything like that. And no, he's not cheating on me, or me on him. And no, we're not unhappy with each other either."

On this last statement, Jennifer gave her an odd look. "So, what can possibly be the problem? You both sound happily married to me. Much happier than lots of couples I know."

"Well, you know that part of the reason I've been working from home is because I'm trying to get pregnant . . ."

Jennifer nodded. "Yes, and I've always told you it doesn't matter a bit. I was working as a barmaid when I got pregnant with Ashley." She laughed. "Okay, maybe that's not the best recommendation I can give you—for all I know, that may be why she turned out so weird. But I'm sure you know what I mean."

"Yes, I do." Maryanne decided to just come out with it. "Well, the problem is, Bob and I aren't having much sex nowadays."

Jennifer's eyes widened. "But why not? You're both young, fit, and attractive. I wouldn't imagine sex to be a problem for either of you." Then her eyes narrowed almost to slits. "No, don't tell me you're in one of those modern asexual situations. You know, when someone just completely loses interest in lovemaking? Seems to be happening a lot nowadays."

Maryanne shook her head. "No, it's not that at all. I'm more than ready to have sex with Bob. In fact, sometimes I'm so horny, even using my vibrator is no good. But Bob is simply too *tired* to perform in bed."

Jennifer's surprise was clearly written on her face. "He can't get it up? But he isn't even thirty yet. Neither of you are."

Maryanne shook her head and gave a little laugh. "No, he can still get it up. We've no problems in that department. The problem is that Bob is so overworked at work at the moment that, once he gets in through the door, which nowadays is always at ten or eleven o'clock each night, he kisses me goodnight, walks straight through into our bedroom and falls asleep, sometimes without even bothering to take his shoes off. Most nights, he's too tired to eat his dinner. In fact, recently I even stopped making dinner and Bob doesn't even notice."

Realizing that they had both finished their coffee now, Jennifer gestured out through the kitchen entrance. "Hey, let's go sit in the living room."

Maryanne got up and walked out ahead of Jennifer, saying over her shoulder, "So, as you can imagine from what I've just told you, with Bob that tired when he gets home each night, and with his needing to dash out again early every morning, there's no time in-between for sex." She sat in an armchair near the television and stared at Jennifer, who was also sitting down. "It's crazy how they've got Bob working all through the weekend too; hardly a moment's rest. And meanwhile, I haven't gotten laid in . . . I mean this without exaggerating . . . a month." She scowled. "The last time we tried to do it, he fell asleep immediately after sticking it in me."

"Considering that he's not cheating on you, and you know exactly *why* he's so tired, I don't see too much of a problem." Jennifer laughed. "I mean, thank God for vibrators, right?"

But Maryanne shook her head. "You're missing the point. Sex toys are great when you aren't in a relationship; but they make a really poor substitute when you have a lover and are deeply in love with that person."

"Tell me about it," Jennifer agreed with a morose glance in the direction of the hallway that led to her own bedroom, where her own stroke-invalided husband lay in bed.

"And also, vibrators can't get you pregnant," Maryanne went on. "Yes, I know it's unreasonable and irrational, but I keep feeling like time is running out for me and I need to be pregnant with a baby already."

"I can understand that," Jennifer said. "But I don't see what you're so worried about. You guys still have that trip to Mexico planned, don't you?"

Maryanne nodded. "Yes, but our departure date is still a month off. I can't help but feel that I'll go crazy if Bob doesn't make love to me for the next month."

"Why is he so busy anyway?" Jennifer asked.

Maryanne laughed. "The devil's bad luck. First of all, Bob's immediate boss got fired and Bob was drafted in to cover for him until they found a replacement, which they then decided not to do when they saw how good a job Bob was doing replacing the guy they'd fired. But then the guy who was hired to fill Bob's now vacant position got involved in a road rage incident and shot someone, so his job became vacant again, and because they hadn't yet gotten anyone else to fill that slot, Bob had to do both jobs at the same time. And then the branch manager died and so . . . ." Maryanne looked at her friend. "Do you see what I mean by the devil's bad luck?"

Jennifer nodded. "Yes, I do. Except that it's extremely unlikely, I'd almost suspect someone has hexed your husband to work himself to death."

"Anyway, that's my current marital situation," Maryanne finished. "I need help. Like I said, I'm sure I'll go nuts if Bob doesn't resume making love to me soonest." She stared across the room at her friend, and her voice was plaintive when she asked: "Can you help me, Jennifer? Can any of your magic spells help me out here?"

Jennifer didn't reply for a long moment, but then she said, "Hey, I thought you didn't believe in all this mystic and magic stuff?"

"I still don't believe in it," Maryanne cautiously agreed. "But at this juncture I'm so desperate that I'll try anything. And you're always claiming that you can cast spells to influence people's behavior and stuff like that. If you really can do that, I'd like you to do it on my behalf."

Jennifer smiled creepily. " Alright, girl, it's time to make a believer in magic out of you."

CHAPTER 3

After leaving Jennifer's condo, Maryanne felt both relieved and optimistic.

Jennifer has guaranteed me a solution to my problems. I told her all I want is a potion or a spell to give Bob long-lasting erections while he sleeps, so I can ride him to my heart's content, but . . . she's promised me something much better.

Jennifer had however not explained what that 'something much better' was. This mysterious omission bothered Maryanne a little bit, but she shrugged it off.

So long as I'm able to have sex with my darling again and neither of us are harmed by my doing so, I'll be fine with whatever spell she casts.

As she stepped past the elevator to the third-floor landing Maryanne reflected on the fact that she hadn't seen Ashley Haskins's boyfriend Tony for quite a while.

He probably just grew tired of her and broke it off, she concluded while staring at Ashley's front door. *Most likely, he ran for his sanity. Fled our building for a while till she accepts the fact that it's over between them.*

The loud music previously coming from Ashley's condo had stopped now, and yet a sense of strangeness still lingered behind the young woman's door.

Now this is weird, Maryanne thought while standing on the second step from the top, and with the fingers of her right hand tracing circles on the stairway banister. *Why it is that, even though Jennifer dabbles in witchcraft, she doesn't give me a creepy vibe, but her daughter does? And as far as I can tell, Ashley knows next to nothing about magic.*

She moved on quickly, before the condo's blonde inhabitant stepped out through the door, as the shutting off of the music in her living quarters seemed to indicate that she might.

According to Jennifer, Ashley does IT work from home, building creepy websites for weirdos.

While descending the stairs, Maryanne returned her thoughts to herself.

So now, I just need to get those things Jennifer requested . . .

Maryanne opened the door of her own home and walked in.

After getting herself a glass of water from the kitchen, she sat in the living room and thought some more:

It's a good thing I didn't go along with Jennifer's suggestion that we simply cast a spell to reduce Bob's office workload. Doing so would be certain to have a negative effect on his career. Heavy as his workload is now, it's only temporary, and is certain to only last until capable people are employed to fill those two vacant positions and relieve Bob of the extra work he's doing himself at the moment.

She patted her crotch, which now felt both heavy and tender in a pleasant and demanding way.

Dammit. Discussing all that sex with Jennifer has gotten me feeling hornier than a unicorn. And since there's no chance of Bob handling his business tonight . . .

Cursing the oddness of the situation she now found herself in, Maryanne Wilson got up and walked into the bedroom to get her vibrator.

CHAPTER 4

While pulling into the Touchpad Court parking lot in his white pickup truck, Robert Wilson wondered how what had initially seemed like a blessing could have disguised so many curses.

I've been promoted to carry the weight of the world on my shoulders.

That was how it seemed anyway. Sure, like everyone else who worked at E.D.I.T (a.k.a. Ellis Drake Industrial Technology), Bob Wilson had been relieved to learn that Joe Lawrence had gotten the boot. It wasn't anything personal, but Joe was a toxic sort of person, the sort of loudmouth exec who got in everyone's way and prevented them from getting any work done, while at the same time not doing any work of his own.

Most people at E.D.I.T had wondered how the bastard had escaped being laid off for so long, and how such an unqualified ostrich had been promoted so high up in the first place.

But whatever the reason, Joe's incompetence had finally translated into his being given a golden handshake and told to drive off into the far distance.

Good riddance, of course. Except that Joe Lawrence's incompetence as an executive had created massive inefficiency issues in the business. Things that should run smoothly behaved epileptically, while unimportant stuff worked without flaws.

As a fellow E.D.I.T staffer had explained it: "It's like Joe set things up to function perfectly at his level of ineptitude, and now that he's left us, his insane business model is about to fall apart because *we* know what we're doing."

And E.D.I.T falling apart wasn't something anyone at the company wanted to happen. Everyone had invested too much time and energy into the business to let it go bust; and most of them had mortgages and had purchased stock options, which, if the rug got pulled from beneath their feet, could result in the kind of mass suicidal behavior unheard of since the Great Depression.

And so, since Joe left two months ago, Bob Wilson had been occupied with plugging the leaks and setting Mr. Ellis Drake's company to rights again, which had initially been easy enough. Until . . .

But then that idiot Finch had to go and shoot someone over a parking space. Shit!

Finch pulling that piece of madness had meant Bob was suddenly doing two people's work—both fixing Joe Lawrence's massive business potholes, and also managing his previous job, while the company struggled to find a replacement who didn't have the sort of mental health issues the now jailed Mike Finchley had had.

And then, just last week, old Dave had to go and die on us, and I'm now saddled with his workload too . . .

Which had been the proverbial last straw.

Bob parked his car, killed the ignition, and then tried to relax for a few seconds. He stopped after realizing it wasn't working. He seemed to have forgotten how to relax.

He flipped down the sun visor and checked out his reflection in its mirror: red eyes with bags of flesh underneath them; and yet those same exhausted eyes beamed out a terrifying caffeinated vitality. Nowadays, relaxation was anti-survival—too much could go wrong at work in the five or ten minutes it would take Bob to unwind and recharge his mental batteries. Best he remain wired on caffeine—a constant diet of Death Wish coffee—and surf over each successive crisis.

Up till last month, I'd never have believed anyone could be this overworked, Bob thought, finally hauling his laptop bag over from the Ford's front passenger seat and clicking his door open. He felt completely exhausted, out before he'd even gotten onto his feet, and once more thanked God he'd not skewed off the highway and killed someone on his way home. All he could think about now was falling into bed and waking up tomorrow morning to start the whole exhausting process again.

Thank heavens that Maryanne and I have that vacation down in Acapulco coming up. That's if I've not suffered a nervous breakdown by then.

Bob climbed out of the truck, locked it, and began walking towards the front entrance to the condo building.

"Hey, Bob, wait up!"

Bob turned to see who was calling. He hid his unease on seeing it was Ashley Haskins. Ashley was just getting out of her own car, a silver Honda. Bob had been so locked up in his thoughts that he'd not noticed her arriving in the parking lot after him.

This had been happening a lot these past few weeks. Bob would get lost in thought, usually about how tired he was, and then suddenly realize he'd lost track of what was happening around him. The weird thing, however, was that this never happened at work, or, thankfully, while he commuted to and from the office.

I hope I'm not slowly turning into the sort of nut Finch was!

He waited for Ashley to join him.

Ashley Haskins was very attractive. Platinum blonde like her invalided father, she was tall for a woman, had a good figure and a lovely face. But whenever Bob looked at her, he also saw something indefinable in her facial expression; something that unsettled him because he didn't understand it.

Something just isn't right about this woman, Bob thought for possibly the hundredth time as Ashley approached him now, clutching several packed grocery bags to her ample breasts. Bob wondered why she was out shopping so late at night, since she worked at home and could have gone out earlier in the day; or simply ordered her groceries online.

"Hey, you still working odd hours?" Ashley asked once she reached him, then peered closely into his eyes. "Man, you look dead on your feet."

Bob managed to laugh. "Each day when I arrive at the office in the morning, I imagine I now know what hell must be like—sixteen hours of non-stop work a day."

Ashley nodded, her blue eyes bright. "Like that meme: 'Eat, sleep, repeat?' "

"In my case it's, 'Work till you drop, Die—Repeat.' " He gestured to her grocery bags. "Give you a hand with those?"

Ashley nodded. "Thanks." She handed him two of the bags. "You're a real gentleman, Bob," she said as they walked together towards the building's entrance. "*Too much* of a gentleman, even. Maryanne's one lucky woman."

"Hey, I haven't seen Tony around lately," Bob quickly replied to change the subject.

But Ashley wasn't to be dissuaded. "Tony? Oh, he's been around; you're just working different shifts, that's all." Because Bob was helping her carry some of her grocery purchases, it was left to her to unlock the building's front door and she took her time with doing so.

"Why don't you like me, Bob?" she asked, leaning so close to him that their faces almost touched. "We both work in IT—we should be really good friends. I mean, *really* good friends."

"I don't dislike you," Bob hastily said, before her sweet breath blew in his face, and pulled back quickly before her lips brushed his. "But you're forgetting that neither of us are single. I've got Maryanne to consider and you've got Tony."

Ashley had her key in the lock now, but still hadn't yet turned it. "So, you're saying that if we were both single, you'd date me?"

"Yes, yes!" Bob said. "But that won't happen, will it? We're both happy with our partners."

"Well, there's always kisses at Christmas parties," Ashley said playfully. Then she turned the key in the lock so they could both enter the building.

"Let's ride in the elevator together," Ashley suggested.

Seeing as he was helping her with her groceries, this made sense to Bob.

Standing side-by-side in the cage, Bob pondered his weird situation with Ashley Haskins. Ashley had never hidden the fact that she was attracted to him. Indeed, Bob suspected Ashley's liking of him was one of the reasons they'd gotten this condo unit so easy. Ashley's mother Jennifer had told Maryanne that she and Bob had bid lower than some other couples who'd wanted to purchase their particular condo unit.

"But we—Chris and I, and Ashley too—the three of us just had a better feeling about you two than we did about any of the other prospective buyers," Jennifer had said.

Yes, Ashley REALLY likes me. But, since she began dating Tony, she'd stopped acting suggestively to me. So why the sudden about-face? What's happened to Tony all of a sudden? Has he broken up with Ashley? Or has Tony begun seeing some other woman?

The elevator reached the top floor. Bob got out alongside Ashley and walked with her to her front door.

"Care to come inside and have a drink with moi?" she asked teasingly as she slipped her key in the lock.

But Bob shook his head. "I've spent too long with you as it is. If Maryanne heard my truck pull into the court, she'll be wondering what we're doing now."

That comment made Ashley laugh as she pushed her door wide open and stepped inside. "I've a lot of ideas about what we can do together and some of them won't hurt you at all."

Her comment made no sense to Bob, and his face clearly showed it, because she laughed and added: "Relax, Bobby, I'm just joking."

He nodded, suddenly remembering how tired he was and yawning with the bags in his hands. Bob stared beyond Ashley as she stepped inside her condo unit and dropped her bags on a table. His eyes focused on a couch; a piece of furniture that almost magnetically beckoned to him to come lie on it. He forced himself to remain in place and wait for Ashley to return.

"Not that I'm gonna be of any use to Maryanne either tonight in my current condition," he admitted to Ashley as she took her shopping bags from him. "I'm counting the days to my next vacation and then out of the country we both fly."

Ashley nodded. "You really do look out on your feet." She smiled at Bob. "Listen, let's just be friends, okay? No strings attached. You agree to that and I'll not pressurize you any more to have a relationship with me. Like I said, we're both in IT and so, aside from hanging out together from time to time, we can help each other out with work-related stuff."

That seemed harmless enough to Bob. "Alright," he readily agreed, "we're friends now."

"For real?"

"Yeah, for real. We're besties, even."

Ashley grinned at this, then leaned forward and whispered in his ear: "You won't regret this, Bob. You won't ever regret this."

Then she stepped back from him and, still smiling happily, shut her door, leaving him alone in the corridor.

Bob turned around and walked past the elevator to the stairs. He and Maryanne's condo unit was just one floor down, and he didn't want to black out in the elevator and find himself on the ground floor.

He was relieved when he made it through his own front door into his wife's welcoming arms.

Bob stopped thinking about his beautiful new 'bestie' Ashley Haskins the moment he saw Maryanne's lovely face.

CHAPTER 5

Tonight, Bob Wilson was surprised by how warm and welcoming Maryanne was. Of recent she'd been hostile and even difficult at times, particularly when he arrived home this late, which nowadays was most days. But tonight, she seemed delighted to see him, which was a complete contrast to her facial demeanor when he'd left home that morning.

He decided to go with the flow. He had no idea how long his wife would remain in 'sweetness and cream' mode, and felt it was best that he enjoy it while it lasted.

So tonight, Bob kissed Maryanne back as warmly as she kissed him, and managed to smile as she steered his exhausted body towards the dining table. He felt much more tired than hungry, but wanted to please Maryanne because she was being so pleasant herself.

"I've prepared something special for us tonight," she told him on emerging from the kitchen with two steaming plates. "Something you're certain to enjoy."

Bob nodded as she served him. He wasn't certain what the food was, but it tasted delicious and went very well with the red wine that Maryanne served along with it.

He felt apprehensive during the meal, however. The last time Maryanne had been this nice to him, she'd wanted him to perform in bed; and that had been a disaster. According to her angry account the next morning, he had fallen asleep right after he'd penetrated her, and she'd had to recourse to her vibrator to satisfy her.

And tonight, I feel even more tired than I did that night, if such a state is possible. I've zero hopes of getting hard, talk less of sustaining an erection.

But no, to Bob's surprise, tonight Maryanne didn't seem to want sex from him. Once dinner was over, she smiled at him and said, "Wow, darling, you look so tired that I'll soon begin yawning in sympathy with you. How about I see you into the bedroom and get you undressed and you can go to sleep?"

"I'm sorry, hon . . ." Bob apologized as she helped him out of his clothes. "I really wanna make love to you, but . . . shit! Tonight, I'm . . . I'm . . . even more tired than usual."

But Maryanne just smiled understandingly. "That's okay, darling; I understand. You can make it up to me during our upcoming vacation. For tonight, just you lay down and go to sleep."

So, Bob laid down and went to sleep like she told him to, unaware that the reason he felt even more sleepy than usual tonight was because Maryanne had drugged the wine she'd served him with a powder she'd gotten from Jennifer, one that would ensure he wouldn't wake up when she cut him.

Maryanne waited till Bob was snoring soundly, and then opened up her nightstand and got out a pair of scissors, a razor blade, and a pack of Band Aids.

CHAPTER 6

After Bob left for work the next morning, Maryanne went upstairs to visit Jennifer again. She did take the precaution of first waiting for an hour after Bob's departure before leaving their condo, just in case he'd forgotten something he needed for work and came back for it—she didn't want him imagining she spent her days gossiping—but once she was certain he wouldn't be back till nighttime, she called Jennifer on the phone to let her know she was coming up, and then climbed the stairs.

This time Jennifer was attired very differently when she opened the door to admit Maryanne into her condo.

Wow, she ain't fooling around! Maryanne thought on seeing Jennifer's floor-length black robe with its startling decoration of silver moons and crimson pentagrams. Jennifer was also wearing thick black-and-silver makeup.

"Well, come on in," she said.

Maryanne stepped forward into the smell of sweet incense. The heady odor was coming from elsewhere in the house however, as there were no burning joss sticks in Jennifer's living room.

More often than not, Jennifer and Chris's condominium was a cornucopia of weird smells, almost as if the smells were pets or pests prowling through the rooms of this third-floor living space. That barest hint of cinnamon Maryanne smelled might be a mouse, and the other, much stronger and much darker oriental scent overlaying it, the Persian cat chasing the mouse. There were other, much more indefinable scents; snakes and raccoons, even skunks, maybe.

"I really hope I'm doing the right thing here," Maryanne said nervously as she handed both the snips of Bob's pubic hair and little vial of his blood to Jennifer. "I can't stop feeling guilty."

Jennifer smiled understandingly. "It's always that way at first. But the end will definitely justify the means."

"I sure hope so."

"You're a little early. I was still setting up when you arrived." Jennifer gestured across her living room. "Go say hi to Chris out on the balcony, while I finish my preparations."

Maryanne had been so caught up in thoughts of what they were going to do that she'd forgotten Jennifer's invalided husband.

Of course, he'll be home; where else could he be? It's not like creepy Ashley is gonna win any awards for 'Daughter of the Year' by offering to babysit her dad while we're busing doing whatever it is we'll be doing.

Looking out through the drapes now, she could see the rear of Chris's wheelchair, its silver frame glinting in the sunlight.

"Okay," she agreed. "Call me when you're done."

"I will."

Maryanne stepped outside and leaned against the balcony facing Chris Haskins.

"Good morning, Chris," she said.

Chris Haskins slowly turned and looked up at her. He was a large man and filled the wheelchair. Formerly a very active and jovial fellow, the stroke had reduced him to a shadow of his former self. Chris's eyes still projected some of that old vitality, but the constant dribble of spit down the left side of his mouth, running through his pepper-salt-colored beard like a river through a valley, and the uncontrollable twitching of his lips, killed any illusion of strength in him.

The stricken man raised a hand with trembling fingers and waved to Maryanne. "He . . . ey, gi . . . irl," he slowly replied, with his lips twisting up in a caricature of a smile.

She nodded back and patted his hand, not wanting to make him speak any more than he had to. They'd all been good friends before he'd suddenly slumped at work that morning, and so Maryanne didn't feel uncomfortable being alone with him.

Now that they'd exchanged their greetings, Maryanne stood beside him with one hand on his shoulder, staring out over the condominium parking lot. All that was really visible from she and Bob's second-floor residence were trees, trees, and more trees. But up here? Well, the trees hadn't vanished, but she could also make out the giant Walmart Supercenter down on Broadway, and further south, several groups of Taunton high rises.

I really wonder what Chris is thinking now, she thought. *I wonder how it feels to sit in a wheelchair all day waiting to get better, wondering if it will ever happen, and praying desperately that this isn't how he's going to spend the rest of his life—as an invalid entirely reliant on others. Well, Jennifer is loving enough, but Chris must be praying that Jennifer doesn't either die or fall sick herself and leave him or both of them in Ashley's hands.*

Then, either a wind blew, or Chris's wheelchair shifted slightly, and the blanket Jennifer had draped over his legs to keep him warm slipped off them to the floor. Jennifer quickly bent down and retrieved it and rearranged it on Chris's legs, then tucked it in securely. She tried not to look in his face when she did this. She didn't want him to think she was pitying him, or that she wanted his gratitude for doing such a small thing for him.

"Tha-tha-thanks," he said anyway.

And now, as Maryanne listened to Jennifer potter away somewhere in the house and as she and Jennifer's husband both kept their silent vigils on the balcony, Maryanne felt a little weird. It took her a little while to pinpoint the source of her unease.

Yes, that's it! Most stroke cases I hear or read about, people tend to improve with time. But in Chris's case, he seems to be getting worse. When Chris first came back home from the hospital, he could speak a lot better than he does now. He didn't stutter anywhere near as much either; and he could also move his arms better. So, what's the matter with him? Jennifer takes him regularly to the hospital for his checkups and the doctors must know something's not ri—oh, I know what it is! It has to be all the herbal soups Jennifer keeps feeding him. But—

"Hey, you can come in now!" Jennifer called out then.

So, Maryanne leaned over Chris's wheelchair and hugged him, then she hurried off the balcony and into the condo again.

CHAPTER 7

Jennifer led Maryanne out of her living room and into a room that she'd never entered before.

This room was corpse-gray in color and was furnished with five high-backed chairs arranged around a circular central table and two bookcases along opposite walls. However, the room's most striking feature was its black carpet, which, as if it was an extension of Jennifer's robe, was also patterned with silver moons and red pentagrams.

The lighting in here was subdued and spooky. Maryanne felt instantly at unease.

Jennifer, who looked exceptionally creepy now with the spooky lighting shining on her black and silver makeup, shut the door behind them and pointed to the table.

"Relax and have a seat," she said. "You'll see I've been busy with what you brought me."

Maryanne shuddered on seeing the small doll that lay in the middle of the table, which she also now noticed was deeply engraved with six pentagrams, one right in its middle and the other five spaced at equal distances around its rim, each one of these outer five positioned so that it faced a point of the star in the central circle.

She also realized that each of the five chairs placed around the table faced one of the pentagrams.

Also on the table were several books and a deck of obscenely illustrated cards, and also the vial of Bob's blood that she'd collected.

She sat and stared at the doll. The doll lay in the central pentagram. It was made of carved wood, was about six inches long, and was featureless other than for the inch-long erect penis that marked it as male, around the base of which had been glued a thick clump of brown hair; hair that Maryanne immediately recognized as that which she'd snipped off Bob's crotch last night while he slept his drugged sleep.

Oh, so that's what it was for! Maryanne thought with a thrill of both excitement and dread. *Okay, so what's the blood for?*

The vial of blood stood next to the doll. Jennifer, who had now seated herself opposite Maryanne, picked up the doll and twisted its head off. Maryanne saw that the little carved figurine was hollow inside. Next, Jennifer picked up the vial of blood, unstopped it, and poured its red content into the doll. Then she screwed the doll's head back onto its shoulders again and discarded the vial of blood into a trash can under the table.

"Now, let's do some magic," she said with a smile.

Maryanne nodded breathlessly. For some reason, she'd suddenly begun feeling wet between her legs. She felt convinced that Jennifer would succeed in what she was about to do.

The first weird thing that happened now was that Jennifer put the blood-filled doll back on the table and it stood upright. Curious about this, Maryanne reached out a hand and tried to push the doll over onto its side again, but it wouldn't budge.

She looked nervously up at Jennifer. "Why do I feel so horny?" she asked in a pathetic voice. "Right now, I feel like I'd readily fuck Satan himself."

Before replying, Jennifer reached below the table with her left hand. Maryanne watched her pull up her long robe and swipe her fingers between her thighs. When she next showed her hand to Maryanne, her fingers were wet with her sexual juices.

"You're not alone. I'm horny too. Our being in this state is natural because we're performing a sexual ritual. If we were men, we'd both have rock-hard cocks now."

Maryanne blushed at the sight of her friend's sex-slicked fingers. "But we've not begun performing the ritual yet. Right?"

Jennifer dried her fingers on her robe. "Wrong. The ritual began the moment we both sat down."

"Oh." Then, when Jennifer didn't do or say anything more for a few moments, Maryanne boldly asked: "Hey, how do you take care of yourself sexually now that Chris is bedridden? I can imagine you haven't gotten laid yourself since he had his . . ."

Jennifer's reply was to laugh at the question. "What makes you think I haven't gotten laid since then?"

Maryanne's eyes widened. This was news to her. "Er . . . have you?"

Jennifer smirked at her. "Let's finish the ritual. We can play truth or dare later."

Feeling somewhat chastened, Maryanne nodded. "I was just curious, you know."

Jennifer didn't reply, but instead picked up one of the books on the table, and flipped open its pages. After scanning through it for a while, she nodded to herself, put the book down again, and nodded at Maryanne.

"Alright," she said. "Now, place one hand on your vagina, and touch the doll with the other. Some weird stuff is going to happen now, but don't be afraid; it's all in a good cause."

Maryanne nodded and did as she was told. She was dripping between the legs now; her panties were drenched and the moisture was seeping through the crotch of her denim shorts. In a few seconds her fingers were embarrassingly sticky.

Jennifer began laughing. "That's why I'm not wearing panties myself."

Then the witch woman's mirth abruptly ended. "Alright, time to get serious," she said.

Assuming the same position as Maryanne—left hand on crotch, right hand on doll—Jennifer began chanting some weird abracadabra stuff that sounded like Latin.

"Boku Krek, Boku Krek . . . !"

Maryanne concentrated. The room had begun feeling strange. The doll too had begun feeling strange. The figurine suddenly felt like it was flesh and blood, not wood.

Then Jennifer stopped chanting. Immediately her voice fell silent, the lights in the room all went out and the doll began glowing a bright red beneath she and Maryanne's fingers.

"Don't break contact with the doll," Jennifer warned Maryanne, a moment before the latter would have done so. "It happens now. Keep your eyes open too. See and believe."

Maryanne would have preferred to keep her eyes shut. The combination of gushing wetness between her legs, with its corresponding upward spiral of sexual desire, and the throbbing phallic state of the doll on the table were almost too much for her to cope with.

At least if I shut my eyes, I can pretend that none of this is happening.

But she obeyed Jennifer and kept her eyes open. And just when she felt like she would swoon from the intensity of the lust she felt consuming her, she saw a red door open . . . somewhere.

That was the thing: Maryanne couldn't pinpoint exactly where in time and space the red door was opening. What she could see however, was that wherever it was, was a very hot place indeed. And then she saw a dark form emerging through the red door. The form was humanoid, but seemed to have horns, and maybe bluish skin also.

From being infinitely far away, suddenly the bluish humanoid form was right there in the room with them, and the room itself now stank of sulfur or rotten eggs. And then the next moment, the form was no longer there and Maryanne felt a burst of heat beneath her fingers which made her at last jerk them away from the glowing wooden doll.

Jennifer felt the heat too and also instinctively jerked back her hand; but her garishly illumined face now had a smile of success on it.

Then the lights came on again, just in time for Maryanne to watch the doll disintegrate into a pile of ash on the table. Soon, the ash was all there was to view; no sign of wood or blood remained at all.

Maryanne gaped at Jennifer, who was watching her. "What just happened?"

"Nothing to worry about," the witch replied. "We've just improved your sex life about a hundred-fold."

Maryanne found that she could now relax. In the same way that the smell of rotten eggs in the room was already fading away, her own burning lust was lowering to manageable levels again. "So how does this work?" she asked.

"Simple enough," Jennifer explained. "All I've done is provide your husband with a demonic sexual helper. It'll lay dormant during the daytime . . . but at night. I mean once he's asleep, it'll take over." She winked at Maryanne. "Buckle up, girl, you're in for quite a ride, going forward from tonight."

"Huh?" Maryanne gaped at her. "What? That thing we saw . . . it's gonna have sex with me?"

"Well, what do you expect it to do—buy you flowers and take you out on dates?" Jennifer laughed at her friend's confusion for a short while. "No, no, no, it won't have sex with you in its own form. It's going to be in your husband's body. It'll help him satisfy you, that's all." She sighed as if a sudden wave of tiredness had fallen on her. "You really won't be able to tell the difference. No, no . . . that's wrong, there is one major difference between them."

"I hope you're not talking about dick size. I don't want some giant demon dick. I'm fine with Bob's dick. I just . . ."

Jennifer shook her head. "It's not that. I just remembered how you can tell them apart. The demon has red eyes. So, when your husband's normally blue eyes are red—red like the doll was shining just now—that means the demon is running his body. But at other times, no. He'll still be your regular overworked Bob."

Maryanne struggled to take all this in. For someone who hadn't actively believed in the afterlife till five minutes ago, it was a lot to absorb. Previously, where Maryanne had been concerned, God, devils, and angels were stuff for priests to worry about; and churches were places where one first got married and was later buried. But her sexual desperation had brought her to this point and there was no way she wasn't going to give it her best shot.

"And Bob won't be hurt in any way?" she cautiously asked. "You're certain he won't suffer any harm? The demon won't harm him."

"Not at all."

"And he won't find out either?"

"Not unless you tell him what both of us just did." Jennifer got to her feet. "Look, let's go drink some coffee in the kitchen, and I'll make us both sandwiches as well. Casting spells is hungry work."

Nodding and feeling glad that she was going to have some sex at last, Maryanne followed Jennifer out of the 'magic room,' and down the hallway to the kitchen.

She however couldn't stop wondering what sex with a demon (in her darling husband's body, of course) would be like.

It had better be really damn good, she thought, staring down at the completely soaked crotch of her denim shorts, then peeking out onto the balcony at the motionless man in the wheelchair. *At the moment I'm glad Chris is out there, or else he'd think Jennifer and I had been making out in one of their bedrooms!*

"I almost forgot to ask you," Jennifer said, while getting sandwich stuff out of her fridge, "how did you explain the cut on Bob's arm to him this morning? He'd have realized he didn't fall asleep wearing a Band Aid."

Maryanne shrugged. "That part was easy. I told him I spilled a pack of razor blades on the bed and missed one when I gathered them up again." She smiled. "He even thanked me for bandaging him up. Then he leapt out of bed, got dressed, and dashed out the front door to the office."

Jennifer burst out laughing.

CHAPTER 8

An orphan herself, and with her only surviving relative being a senile old uncle in a retirement home, Maryanne Wilson was looking forward to being a mother. And so, she was making what she considered to be adequate preparations for the great lifechanging event.

And this was one of the reasons why, even though she knew she could continue working through her pregnancy, she'd decided she didn't want to. Bob currently earned enough money for both of them, in addition to which, in the three years of their marriage before deciding she'd rather be a stay-at-home-mom, Maryanne had actively saved a fair amount of money herself, to help she and Bob over any initial rough patches when the babies began coming.

Of course, with Bob's new promotion, they no longer needed that saved money, but it was a good nest egg to have, just in case.

Though Maryanne still did some customer-care work from home, nowadays she preferred to spend her time getting used to being at home alone, understanding that her periods of inactivity didn't make her any less of a useful person and that being a mother was as much of a career (and just as much work) as going out to an office.

With her first baby not yet arrived or even on its way yet, Maryanne discovered she spent most of her day either watching soaps or on social media.

Still, she viewed this positively too. She intended that once she was pregnant, she would begin a vlog of her pregnancy, where she (with occasional guest appearances from her next-condo neighbor Amanda Fenton) would update her followers on the event's nine-month progress.

She was pleased that Bob supported her in all this.

Their neighbor Amanda Fenton was twenty-seven, the same age as Maryanne, and was also trying to get pregnant, which gave them a lot in common and lots to talk about. Maryanne almost considered Amanda to be her best friend.

CHAPTER 9

That night, Bob staggered in as tired as usual.

"I really don't see why it's so hard to replace Finch," he complained to Maryanne as they ate dinner. "I'm only twenty-eight, but at this rate I'll likely wind up having a stroke like Chris did."

"Don't exaggerate, darling," Maryanne said, with a broad smile.

"I like it that you're able to smile about something," Bob went on, jerking his tie off of his neck like it was strangling him, then staring in contemplation at the Band Aid on his left hand as if he'd just realized it was there and was wondering what it was. "Honey, you've been gloomy for way too long." He drank some water and shook his head. "Yeah, yeah, I know it's my fault. I've not had any quality time for you; and that's twice as bad now that you're no longer working, so you've no distractions except the internet. But . . . but . . . but trust me, honey. I'm almost done sorting out Joe's messes, and even if I don't get through with that, the date on which I start my vacation has officially been confirmed. That's one month from today. And then I'm on vacation for a whole month. So, we'll have a full month to ourselves."

Maryanne stabbed her steak and smirked. "A whole month? Sweetheart, are you sure Ellis Drake Industrial Technology can spare you for that long? Won't E.D.I.T have edited itself out of existence— have crumbled and gone bankrupt—before we get back?"

Bob missed her sarcasm. "Honey, the directors all agree that I've been overworking myself and that if they haven't found a suitable replacement, at least for Finch by then, they'll let Henley take over and overwork him too."

Maryanne laughed at that. "Henley's old and fat. With your current workload, he's likely to die from a coronary before we return from Acapulco."

"Better him than me. I just want this crap phase of our lives to be over with." Bob frowned. "You, know, I ran into Rodney downstairs just now and he was lamenting how I never come around to drink beers or watch the game at his place anymore. I miss that. I even miss those times when that lout Marvin's around."

Maryanne laughed some more and pretended interest.

***

Rodney Sherrick lived downstairs, in the flat directly below theirs, and could maybe qualify as Bob's best friend. Marvin on the other hand, lived next door and was Amanda's boyfriend, and while Amanda and Maryanne got along very well, Bob tended to shy away from Marvin's company, mainly because Marvin was a giant biker guy who always tried to intimidate men smaller in stature than himself.

As Bob regularly told Maryanne, "I get pushed around enough at work. I don't need that crap at home too."

However, the three men, along with Jennifer's husband Chris (back when he'd been in good health), and Ashley's boyfriend Tony Barbosa, who rented the downstairs condo beneath Amanda and Marvin's, had regularly gotten together, usually in Rodney's place.

Rodney's place was the men's preferred mecca for three reasons.

Firstly, because Rodney Sherrick had the biggest TV set in the building. Rodney had one of those giant wall-to-wall models, the sort that made you imagine you'd died and heaven was a cinema hall.

Secondly, Rodney, who half-owned a video store, also had a massive collection of DVDs, which included lots of porn.

And thirdly, and most important of all, even though Rodney claimed he wasn't gay, the guy had neither a wife nor a girlfriend who could bitch about them invading her living space and kick them out, which made Rodney's pad the ideal place for the other men in the building to gather to escape their own wives and girlfriends, or to just get roaring drunk and watch the NFL game.

***

Maryanne ate slowly, wishing that dinner would soon be over, so she could see if Jennifer's witchcraft had really worked. To make conversation, she asked: "Baby, have you run into Tony lately? Either when you're leaving for work, or arriving back home? I haven't seen him in two weeks."

Bob, who was just finishing his steak, shook his head. Regarding Maryanne through puffy exhausted eyes, he shook his head. "Nope, haven't seen him either. But I did run into Ashley last night and she says he's around, it's just our schedules that clash."

"Yes, I guess that's right," Maryanne replied in a disinterested voice, while mentally willing her husband to rise from the table and shamble off to bed and fall soundly asleep, so that she could then instead rouse the demon in his body to make love to her.

And then, suddenly, dinner was over, and with a sigh, Bob headed for the bedroom.

"Sorry, hon, but I'll make all this lovemaking you're missing up to you during our vacation," Bob called back over his shoulder as he vanished through the bedroom doorway.

"That's alright, baby," Maryanne replied.

Then, figuring she needed to give him enough time to get undressed and fall asleep, she took her time with clearing away the dishes and loading up the dishwasher.

Then, she headed for the bedroom.

To her disappointment, Bob wasn't yet asleep, he was just getting undressed.

Oh no! she thought in intense sexual frustration. *Jennifer's magic didn't work!*

But then, Bob looked over at Maryanne and smiled, and that was when she realized that her husband's eyes were red, not blue; a bright and glowing red. Meaning Jennifer's spell had worked, and that this 'Bob' was the other one—the sex-demon-energized one. So clearly, what had happened was that her husband had fallen asleep in his clothes, and now the demon lover wanted out of them.

This welcome realization made Maryanne draw in a sharp intake of breath. And her heart thumped hard against her ribcage when she noticed that when 'Bob' slipped off his pants, his penis was hard, sticking up proudly in a way she'd not seen it behave in a month.

That was enough for Maryanne.

"Oh yeah!" she yelped and then quickly shed her clothes and hurried over to play with her living sex toy.

CHAPTER 10

The next morning, Bob got up, made his normal complaint of how tired he was even after getting some rest, ate some breakfast, and then dutifully kissed Maryanne on the cheek and headed off to work.

This version of Bob was of course the everyday 'blue-eyed' Bob.

After he'd left home, Maryanne remained sitting at the dining table for a full hour, reviewing the previous night.

Oh, holy fuck. No, maybe, that should be unholy fuck!

Maryanne still couldn't believe how great the sex had been. 'Bob' had been inexhaustible—a total sex machine. She thought they'd made love five times, or maybe it was six—Maryanne wasn't sure, because after a while her orgasms had blurred into one another until she'd passed out from the sheer ecstasy of them.

And then she'd woken up to find 'Bob' was still thrusting into her, his penis moving like a fleshy piston inside of her tender and sopping flesh.

She felt herself between the legs now. *Ouch, I'm a little sore. But it was worth it. It was odd though, the way he never said a word to me all night.*

That was seemingly another way to distinguish between them: the demon 'Bob' never spoke. While Maryanne wouldn't go so far as to describe their style of communication as telepathy, she did know that the demon seemed to understand her every thought before she expressed it. And similarly, she understood its unstated thoughts too, on more than one occasion replying 'Yes' to the unstated question of if she wanted cunnilingus, and 'no' to a similar question about desiring to be fucked in the ass.

Finally, she'd told the demon that she'd had enough, and it had immediately withdrawn from her body, and turned its back to her. Barely seconds later, she understood from the snores beside her that the demon had packed itself back to where it resided during the daytime and her husband was once more back in control of his body.

And so here I am now, she thought. *I'm more sexually satisfied than I've been in months, and yet I don't feel any guilt about it.*

That was honestly weird. *But well, why should I feel guilty anyway? I'm not cheating on Bob. The man I had sex with last night was my husband Bob . . . only he's not aware that it happened.*

Her cellphone rang then. Maryanne grinned when she saw the caller was Jennifer.

"So, how was last night?" Jennifer asked.

"Oh, it was fantastic," Maryanne gushed. "It was still Bob, but it was Bob like I'd always wished he'd be in bed, confident and patient, and yet knowing exactly what I wanted without me even saying a word."

"I told you you'd like it," Jennifer said. "And now on to my payment."

"Payment?" Maryanne said in a surprised voice. "What payment?"

"Now you must sign over your soul to Satan," Jennifer said in a frosty voice. "Or no more juicy orgasms for you . . . ever again in your lifetime!"

Maryanne felt like someone had just shoved an icicle up her butt. "What? Hey, you never said anything about me signing a contract with the devil!"

"One never does. You wanted great sex, and my dark lord gave you what you wanted. Now all he wants in return is your insignificant soul."

Maryanne felt frozen, as if she no longer just had an icicle in her anus, but her whole body had just become one.

"We're waiting," Jennifer cackled over the phone in a creepy voice that sounded stitched together from Maryanne's childhood fears. "Satan and I are waiting—just for you, darling." She began tittering like a TV witch.

By now Maryanne's shock had subsided a little. She felt like crying. *I have to sign a contract with the devil just to have sex? Oh, my dear God, what have I gone and gotten myself into?*

But then Jennifer burst out laughing. "Relax, I'm just kidding. We're friends, so you don't owe me anything. But that's how it always is in the movies, right?" Jennifer sighed over the phone. "Anyway, consider the fright I just gave you payback for the times you said I was full of shit with my talk about magic."

On hearing this, Maryanne almost fell sideways out of her chair in relief.

"Okay, I'm deservedly chastised," she said. "I'm really sorry I didn't take this stuff seriously before."

"But how was it really? How do you feel this morning?"

"I feel great, like I used to during my honeymoon. Back then, sex felt like traveling to heaven while still alive." Then Maryanne's brow furrowed. "I'm quite sore, though. Is it gonna be like this every night?"

"Well, the demon will be there until I remove it, but you only have to have sex when you want to. The demon won't rape you. If you're not in the mood to make love, just say so, and it will pack itself away again."

"Hey, I've a question."

"You need to hurry. I think I hear Ashley knocking the front door. Yeah, it is her. What do you want to know?"

"No rush, I'll ask you later."

"Okay, till later then. Rest your pussy."

Jennifer hung up. Maryanne grinned at the 'rest your pussy' comment. She'd been about to ask Jennifer if this was what Jennifer had meant yesterday, when she'd asked Maryanne why Maryanne had assumed she'd not had any sex since Chris had his stroke.

Okay, because if she did the same thing to Chris that we did to Bob, it's no wonder that he isn't getting better. Imagine an ill man like that having sex all night long, the way 'Bob' and I just did!

Maryanne didn't know whether to be horrified or amused by the thought. Still undecided about it, she got to her feet and humming happily, began clearing away the breakfast things.

CHAPTER 11

And so, with Robert Wilson none the wiser as to what was going on each night, his wife continued happily enjoying his sexual services over the next month.

The longer that this weird one-sided sexual affair continued, the more relaxed Maryanne became. She kept on sleeping with her 'surrogate husband' or 'avatar husband' (as she soon came to think of the demonic 'Bob') and seeing as no harm was coming to the real Bob, she soon ceased worrying about it.

Her real husband meanwhile, though still making no attempt to approach her in bed, had begun complaining less and less of being tired as their planned vacation trip to Acapulco grew nearer.

Bob and Maryanne booked their flights and four-star hotel, planned their sightseeing itinerary, and as their departure date drew closer, packed their luggage.

And then, with just four days remaining before the happily married couple were due to depart for Mexico, Maryanne Wilson made the shocking discovery that her period was late.

Maryanne at first told herself she had no cause for alarm and would surely start bleeding any day now. But when, two days later, her period still hadn't still knocked on her vaginal lips, she realized she might have a problem.

Up to this point in time she had still been enjoying the surrogate Bob's exceptional sexual services on a nightly basis, with some regret that now that her husband would soon have time for her again, he might not measure up to his demonic counterpart in bed.

The next morning was a Thursday. Once Bob headed for work on what was to be his last day at the office for a month, Maryanne got into her car and drove down to the nearest pharmacy, where she purchased several different home pregnancy tests.

CHAPTER 12

Maryanne Wilson stared at the four pregnancy test results in horror. Just to make absolutely sure, she had used them after the other.

Oh, hell no! I can't be pregnant. I simply can't be!

As Maryanne's disbelief congealed to the realization that she had a massive problem on her hands, her mind replayed what she'd told Jennifer, back when Jennifer had advised her to use some kind of family planning protection.

"Demon sex definitely has its perks," Maryanne had said back then with great delight. "One thing I absolutely love is how he never comes inside of me, so there's no mess to clean up afterwards. No ejaculations also mean there's no chance of me getting pregnant. Sure, I really do want to get pregnant for Bob; but how can I possibly explain falling pregnant, if he's not having sex with me that he's aware of?"

"Listen, I know you say he never comes inside you," her older friend had cautioned, but one can never be too careful with these things. All it takes is one slip-up, and you're gonna have a real mess on your hands. Hey, don't come running to me when Bob starts suspecting you're cheating on him."

Back then Maryanne had laughed Jennifer's advice away. That airy certainty seemed so far away now.

I'm pregnant! That's a huge oops. Now, what the hell do I do?

Once Maryanne had calmed down a little, she realized her problem wasn't as bad as she was making it out to be.

Leaving the pregnancy test dipsticks in the bathroom, Maryanne went to the kitchen to make herself some coffee and do some thinking.

Okay, so I'm preggo. It's not the end of the world. I'm at least sure Bob is the baby's daddy; all I need to do is figure out a good explanation as to why junior popped out early. Actually, if I'm not more than two weeks pregnant, I may not have to explain the discrepancy at all. Yeah, so I simply won't tell Bob that we're expecting till I'm at least three months gone and then I'll say I wasn't sure at first and didn't want any false alarms.

She sighed. *Now that I'm certain I'm pregnant, I'll have to discuss this with Jennifer too. Oh, how she's going to make fun of me. There's no escaping that. Particularly since I need to have her remove the demonic sexual helper from Bob's body before we leave for Mexico, or else . . .*

But Maryanne had been so caught up in her thoughts that she'd not heard the front door open. All of a sudden Bob was standing there in the living room, and saying, "Well, honey, I'm all sorted out now for the next month."

"But, but . . ." Maryanne gasped in horror, "you're home early?" Suddenly she was very aware that she'd left her positive pregnancy test results in their bathroom sink.

Bob laughed at her frightened expression. "You look so scared."

"I'm sorry, but you startled me. I wasn't expecting you back this early in the day."

Bob heaved a deep sigh of relief and then dropped his laptop bag on the couch beside her, and began tugging at his tie to loosen it. "That's okay, hon. I just . . ." Then he winced. "Give me a minute to use the bathroom and I'll be back to explain."

And then, with Maryanne's carefully reasoned out plan of pregnancy concealment unraveling before her very eyes, Bob turned away from her and practically ran towards their bedroom and bathroom to pee.

As he vanished down the hallway, Maryanne waited for the storm to break.

I'm so fucked, Maryanne thought. And then the appropriateness of that thought hit her and she smiled sadly. *I'm so, so fucked, it's no wonder I'm pregnant.*

It didn't take long. Bob clearly didn't notice the pregnancy tests until he was done peeing and was washing his hands in the washstand sink; or maybe he noticed them while peeing.

But suddenly, Maryanne heard a loud yell of "WHAT THE FUCK!"

Here it comes, she thought. *Now, he thinks I've been cheating on him.*

Bob emerged from the bedroom door like a dark thundercloud about to burst over the world.

"How long have you been cheating on me?" he demanded, with a tired look on his face. Then he sighed. "Please, Maryanne, don't insult my intelligence by lying about it. I know I haven't slept with you for about two and a half months, and if you're running pregnancy tests on yourself, someone else has most definitely been doing the job for me."

The way he looked while saying this, miserable and defeated by the thought of her imagined infidelity, broke Maryanne's heart.

What the hell have I just gone and done? I really should just have kept my legs closed, she thought as she leapt up and hurried over to him.

"Listen, honey, it's not what you think," she protested, because that was what people in movies always said in such crazy situations and sometimes it seemed to work for them.

Bob was staring at her with pain-filled eyes.

"Listen, I can explain," she said grabbing his arm as he leaned against the hallway entrance. "Believe me, honey, I really can."

But the violence of her husband's response shocked her.

"Get the hell away from me, you damn slut, and go back to your lover!" Bob scowled and then shoved her fiercely away from him.

And this was where things took a turn for the tragic.

Bob had shoved Maryanne away from him with such force that, while backpedaling and trying to right herself, she completely lost her balance, tripped backwards, and then slammed her neck hard into the edge of the dining table.

There was a loud snap as Maryanne Wilson's neck broke. And then she collapsed to the living room floor, stone dead.

CHAPTER 13

Even before Maryanne hit the floor, Bob knew he'd made a grievous mistake by shoving her that hard. But it had been an instinctive response. He'd never hit or even shoved Maryanne before in such a way, but the pain of her betrayal had been so intense that he'd no longer wanted anything to do with her, and his hands had seemingly reacted on their own to protect him from being contaminated by her adulterous touch.

But then she hit the table, and there was that 'crack' like the snapping of a wet branch. And Maryanne's eyes had gaped open at that moment, like she knew something that could never be fixed had broken inside of her body.

And then she'd hit the rug, with her neck bent forward at more than a ninety-degrees angle, and lay still.

Bob ran over to her. "Hey, hey, baby. I'm sorry. I didn't mean to . . ."

But Maryanne wasn't moving at all. Her head was propped upright by a table leg. Bob knelt and gently pulled her away from the table. He was alarmed now by the way Maryanne's neck lolled freely.

Most worryingly, her eyes were wide open, but only the whites of both eyes were visible.

"Hey, honey, wake up! Wake up!"

Bob shook her gently, wondering if he'd need to dial 9-1-1 for help. But when he tried to get her up to a sitting position, her head fell backwards over her shoulders, and that was when the horrible realization hit him that there was nothing paramedics could do now.

She isn't unconscious—she's dead! I've murdered her.

Once Bob understood and accepted that fact, he left Maryanne's corpse where it was and went to sit on the couch. He was trembling with shock and the urge to dial 9-1-1 for help felt almost overpoweringly strong.

But the fact that he was the one responsible for his wife's death put a damper on his enthusiasm to summon law enforcement.

There's no way anyone is gonna believe that I'm innocent. I'll be found guilty and sent to jail. The police are used to this sort of thing happening—husband and wife having a quarrel and then one of them kills the other. They'll think I did it intentionally!

Realizing that he'd begun panicking and needed to calm down again, Bob got up and hurried into the kitchen. His friend Rodney from downstairs had given him a bottle of Wild Turkey whiskey for his last birthday and he searched the kitchen cabinets until he found it.

Not bothering to use a glass, Bob opened up the bottle and took a long slug of the drink. Then he carried the bottle of whiskey back to his living room and sat down again. He leaned back and, staring glumly at Maryanne's corpse, waited for the alcohol to calm him.

When Bob felt that his panic had reduced enough for him to unemotionally analyze his situation, he attempted to do so. But no matter what angle he considered things from, the cold and hard fact still remained that he'd just killed his wife. Accidentally, for sure; unintentionally, definitely; and maybe it would be best for him if he just called the police and told them exactly what had happened.

I should just call the cops right away and get this over with! Maybe they'll even believe me. I'll get a good lawyer and have my day in court. I didn't actually murder Maryanne—this has to be regarded as manslaughter, not murder. But even that comes with a prison sentence.

Bob realized that at the moment he was thinking coldly and logically, more concerned about his own fate than feeling sorry for the death he'd caused. But he understood too that this was because Maryanne had been cheating on him.

All that time I imagined I was depriving her of sex, she's been screwing someone else? Who? I hope it wasn't that meathead Marvin?

A horrible image of Amanda's muscular biker boyfriend bent over Maryanne, naked and sweating and thrusting into her flashed through Bob's head and threatened to reduce him to a senseless rage of tears. There was a gun in the house, and for some desperate moments, only the fact Marvin was unlikely to be at home now prevented Bob from getting the gun out of his nightstand and going to blow Marvin's head off.

He took another long slug of whiskey to calm himself. *Hey, I've no proof Maryanne was sleeping with Marvin! I need to calm down and think rationally.*

Thinking rationally was difficult to do, because the sensible and advisable thing to do in such situations was to call the authorities and get the coroner's office over here to deal with the corpse. Then the detectives would question Bob and decide on his level of culpability in Maryanne's death and whether to press charges against him or not.

It's looking bad, dude. And this morning it was looking great. I really came home early to tell Maryanne I'd gotten a double promotion, that the directors had decided they weren't going to hire anyone else to replace Dave who'd died, but that I'd been promoted to head our section in his place. So, Maryanne and I should be on top of the world now, have gone out to party, and celebrate and tomorrow fly off to Mexico for our sweet vacation. Not . . . not . . . His eyes felt riveted to his wife's corpse. *Definitely not this!*

It was at this point that Bob did begin feeling sorry that he'd killed Maryanne. He took one final drink of whiskey, then dropped the bottle and crawled over to where Maryanne was lying on the floor. He lay down beside her and held her corpse tight. Her body was cold now, and she'd also begun stiffening, but not much.

He kissed her cold face and wept into her blonde hair and whispered: "I'm sorry, honey. I'm really sorry we had to end up like this! You know what, baby? I'm gonna call the cops right now and tell them that I killed you!"

But Bob never got around to calling the police.

Now, Bob Wilson wasn't really any kind of a heavy drinker. The last time he'd had any alcohol in his system was on the night when Maryanne had served him the drugged wine so she could snip off some of his pubic hair and also collect some of his blood for Jennifer.

Add to this the fact that it was only over the last couple of days that Bob's workload at the office had appreciably lessened, meaning that he was still borderline exhausted.

The upshot of this was that the whiskey Bob had drunk soon got the better of him, and while he was weeping and apologizing to his dead wife, he fell asleep.

And then Bob had the strangest dream imaginable.

CHAPTER 14

Bob dreamt that he got up from the living room floor, picked Maryanne's corpse up, and carried it into their bedroom. Once in there, he first stripped off Maryanne's clothes, then got naked himself. With his clothes off he discovered he was sexually aroused, his penis stiff and jerking like it wanted some action.

And then, he parted Maryanne's stiffening legs, spat on her vagina to lubricate her, and inserted himself.

He made love to her hard for several minutes and then came. But he didn't come normal human semen. No, what came out of his cock (which he saw clearly, because there was so much of it that it soon flooded backwards out of Maryanne's pussy) was some sort of blue goo.

Bob kept ejaculating and the blue goo kept squirting out of Maryanne, till it filled the bedroom and he was drowning in it. But then, right before he suffocated, all of the blue goo was sucked up into Maryanne's body, till there was nothing left in the bedroom except that which was smeared on Bob's erection.

CHAPTER 15

Bob groggily woke up. This rousing was at first a slow process. But suddenly he remembered his odd dream and also realized he wasn't in the living room anymore.

"What the hell?"

Bob suddenly realized that he was in bed, in he and Maryanne's bedroom, and that she was in the bed with him and that they were both naked.

Remembering the intimate details of his dream, Bob instantly leapt off the bed. Then he stood beside the bed staring down at his dead wife.

"Oh no, I didn't! Oh, God, please tell me I didn't!"

But apparently, he had. The clear evidence for this was the fact that Maryanne's naked legs, which had previously been tightly held together, were now parted wide, and worse still, that her vaginal opening was distended into a gaping circle, her vaginal muscles no longer possessing the ability to tighten her up again after he'd been inside her.

For Bob's own part, he'd woken up with an erection, which his horror was now causing to deflate. But even stranger, there was a coating of some blue cream or lotion on his penis, which coincided worryingly with the events of his dream . . . no, his nightmare.

Oh, no! I just had sex with my dead wife! Oh my God! How could I do such a thing! First, I killed Maryanne and now . . . now.

Bob felt disgusted, both with himself and with Maryanne, who with her legs bent and parted like that, looked like a fowl being prepared for stuffing. He pulled the blankets over her body to hide her gaping vagina, and then ran into the bathroom to throw up.

After puking, he felt slightly better. Which was when he decided to investigate the blue slime that had been on his penis.

But now, it's all gone! Hey, where the hell did it go?

But then, staring out of the bathroom at the naked corpse in his bed, Bob realized the blue goo was a question for later, if ever.

Oh, my God, am I in such deep shit now. Even if the cops accept the fact that Maryanne's death was accidental, how the hell am I gonna explain that I slept with her after her death? Post mortem lust or what the hell am I gonna say came over me? Or, do I explain it away as the result of my pent-up sexual frustration? Whatever it was, now I'm going to prison for sure.

And Bob knew there was no way, the truth about his necrophilia wouldn't come out, not with the way Maryanne's vagina was currently gaping like a crone's toothless mouth.

The autopsy is certain to reveal everything. I can just see the news headlines!

But sleeping with the corpse made no sense at all to Bob.

For the past two months I've had no libido at all, and even now I don't feel aroused . . . and yet . . . so how in the hell did I fuck Maryanne IN MY SLEEP and not remember it?

Bob left the bathroom, walked past the corpse, and, after pulling on a pair of shorts, went out into to the living room again. Halfway through another drink of whiskey, he shook his head and lowered the bottle from his lips. Then, shaking his head, he returned the bottle of Wild Turkey to its original place in the kitchen cabinet.

The alcohol was responsible for my falling asleep and I can't have any more lapses like that. No slipups. I need to stay sober. I don't want to find myself in bed with Maryanne again, maybe this time having oral or anal sex with her corpse.

Bob returned to the living room to sit down and plan.

One thing's for sure—there's no way I can call the police now. Not after— what's the word the law uses for such acts—yeah, 'desecrating' —not after I've just 'desecrated' Maryanne's corpse. Calling the cops now so will be the biggest mistake of my life. They're gonna throw me in the penitentiary and then throw away the key! The only way I'll ever see the outside world again will be on TV specials about my depravity!

Bob tried to think of a way out of his mess. But no matter how he tried to reason through it, his options were very bad. He had a dead body on his hands, and no way to dispose of it.

And even if I can get rid of Maryanne's body, the cops will soon be asking questions about her disappearance. And then they'll start digging . . . and digging . . . and sooner or later, they'll dig up the evidence I buried, and I'll be in jail with my first parole hearing scheduled for my ninety-ninth birthday. The guys in the office will testify that I've been under a massive amount of stress and pressure lately and I'll be lumped into the same 'nervous breakdown' category with that idiot Finch who shot a guy over a parking space . . .

It seemed hopeless.

41

I could flee to Mexico. The vacation is already planned and everyone knows we're going. But when I don't come back from Mexico and Maryann's corpse is discovered . . . the police will have me deported and . . . same old ending. Oh heck, maybe I should just call the cops and turn myself in anyway!

And it was right then, with his hopes fast dwindling, that Bob heard the noise of a car pulling into the parking lot downstairs and stopping. The sound derailed his train of gloomy thoughts. Wondering if someone had maybe noticed him killing Maryanne and had called the police (which was a ridiculous worry, because even though the living room drapes were parted, no one could possibly have seen what happened from down below), Bob hurried over to the balcony and peered down into the parking lot.

It was just Ashley Haskins returning from somewhere in her silver Honda. Ashley got out of the car and ran for the front entrance because a light drizzle had just begun.

Watching Ashley run set Bob thinking.

Bob realized that, implausible as it might seem from a distance, Ashley Haskins might actually be able to get him out of his current dilemma.

Ashley's help was a desperate hope; but it was the only hope Bob had now.

The problem is, what she's gonna want in return. She'll likely demand all the money I've got now, and will continue milking me dry for the rest of my life. But anything beats going to prison for the rest of my life.

CHAPTER 16

Once Bob had decided to ask Ashley Haskins for help, his mind seemed to thaw back into normalcy. No longer did he feel like he was standing on the verge of a massive precipice, about to fall forward into a deep and endless darkness.

He felt quite certain that Ashley would help him. Hadn't she insisted the last time they'd spoken, that they be friends—besties even—from now on.

Of course, we didn't discuss her becoming an accessory to a murder rap. Because once I don't report Maryanne's death today, I can't imagine any other way that the police are gonna view it. But whatever, I'll simply ask Ashley to help me out, and if she says no, I can still call the cops before evening.

It was midafternoon now. After staring over the balcony for a while longer, Bob got to work.

The first thing he did was move Maryanne's corpse out of the bedroom. Just remembering she was lying in there in their bed made him feel like puking again.

Where to put her body was easily resolved. The condo had a large guest bathroom at the far end of the hallway, where their washing machine was.

But moving Maryanne proved difficult. Each time Bob touched his wife's cold body, he felt an intense revulsion because of what he done to it after her death. This feeling was inescapable, because during the interim when Bob had been making up his mind as to what to do, Maryanne's limbs had all stiffened fully in rigor mortis, locking her legs open and showing Bob the gaping pink evidence of his crime each time he stared between them.

Finally, however, Bob wrapped Maryanne up in a sheet and carried her out to the guest bathroom, where he carefully placed her body in the bathtub. Then, mindful of the fact that she would soon start rotting and stinking, he closed the bathroom window and sprayed half an aerosol can of air freshener into the bathroom.

That should keep the smell in check for a little while, he thought. Holding his breath to keep from choking on the thick aerosol fragrance, he adjusted the sheet he'd wrapped around Maryanne to completely cover her body, and then hurried out of the bathroom and shut the door.

Now that Maryanne was out of sight for a short while, Bob felt some relief. He returned to his bedroom, changed his clothes and left the condo to go talk to Ashley.

CHAPTER 17

Bob took his time with climbing the stairs to Ashley's place. Despite realizing that time wasn't exactly his friend anymore, he was in no hurry to ask for his potential savior's help.

Ashley seemed such a weird type that Bob really had no idea what he was about getting himself into.

While climbing the stairs he heard the sound of his next-door neighbor Amanda leaving her home. Though he was out of view of her condo's door, he knew it wasn't her boyfriend Marvin he was hearing, because after the door shut below him, he heard the fast clicking of a woman's high heels, and Marvin only wore heavy biker boots.

Not feeling like having a conversation with his next-door neighbor, Bob hurried around the turn in the staircase. As he climbed the last few steps he heard the elevator arriving and then opening.

Up on the third floor and faced with Ashley's door, Bob paused one last time to reconsider if he was doing the right thing.

For all I know, Ashley may simply call the cops and hand me over to them.

But deep inside of him, Bob knew Ashley wouldn't turn him in to the police. In addition to his sensing that Jennifer Haskins's daughter had a wild, if not even a very perverse side to her, he also knew she regularly dabbled in illegal stuff.

During Bob's few conversations with Ashley over the course of the year that he and Maryanne had lived here in Touchpad Court, Bob had quickly discovered that Ashley Haskins had a criminal inclination. Their short conversations had revealed that Ashley made her living performing illegal activities online; hacking into the databases of global conglomerates and such like. Ashley had more than once hinted about her dark web connections, and had once openly told Bob that she could get him literally 'Anything he needed online, even if it was a sex slave from Lithuania.'

Bob, who was completely legit with his own usage of the internet, had never corrected Ashley's misinterpretation of the 'I' in his own version of IT to mean 'Industrial' rather than 'Information.' He'd enjoyed misleading her into believing she was speaking to a kindred spirit, a fellow Information Age rebel who was only working for the system to pay the bills.

Bob figured it was time to discover just how deeply connected to the criminal underworld Ashley Haskins really was.

He walked the short distance to her front door and rang her doorbell.

There was a short interval while Ashley most likely put some clothes on, and then peered through the spyhole in the door, then he heard the sound of the chain being slipped off and the door opened.

Ashley hadn't been putting her clothes on. All she had on was a short dress, or maybe she was wearing one of Tony's large tee shirts.

She was surprised to see him. "Bob, what are you doing here? You're the last person I'd have expected to come visit me."

Bob came right out with it: "I've a corpse to dispose of," he told her in a quiet voice. "I don't know exactly why, but I think you can get rid of it for me. I'll pay you whatever you ask."

Ashley at first seemed even more surprised. But then she smiled. Her smile made Bob feel that he'd just slipped his head into a lioness's mouth.

"You'd better come inside then," Ashley said and stepped back from the doorway to admit him into her condo. "Disposing of a corpse isn't the sort of thing we can discuss in the hallway."

Bob peered nervously around her. "Maybe we'd better go down to my place, where we'll be alone."

But Ashley shook her head. "Come on in. I'm the only one home. Tony isn't around."

Feeling equally relieved and worried by her nonchalant acceptance of his confession of murder, Bob stepped into Ashley's home. He didn't really know why, but he really did feel like a fly entering a spider's web.

CHAPTER 18

Ashley's living room was well furnished, but, maybe as spillover from her professional interests, she had an excess of multimedia devices everywhere.

"So, who did you kill?" she asked when they were both seated on her living room couch.

"Maryanne."

Ashley raised her eyebrows. "Yeah, it figures. It's always the wife who gets it. Why did you kill her?"

"She was cheating on me. Listen, it was an accident."

"It always is, man. Lots of similar accidents happen to women each year."

Bob frowned. "Stop judging me. This really *was* an accident. I just shoved her in anger and she . . ."

"And she what?"

"She broke her neck against the edge of the dining table . . . and now . . ." Bob sighed. "And now I've got to somehow dispose of her body or go to jail."

Ashley laughed. "You're only thinking of yourself. You don't seem very remorseful about killing her."

Bob shook his head. "I am *extremely* remorseful, Ashley. I loved Maryanne; I still can't believe she cheated on me. I loved Maryanne so damn much."

"Listen, man, maybe your best bet would be to call the cops. Once they hear how overworked you've been at the office, they're certain to be sympathetic. The most you'll be charged for will be manslaughter. You'll maybe even get a suspended sentence; zero jail time but *years* of community service." Ashley paused and stared coldly at him with her eyes narrowed. "Unless of course, there's something you're not telling me, Bobby."

So, then Bob told Ashley about the necrophilia.

"I still haven't the slightest idea how that happened; I've never had a necrophiliac fantasy in my life," he finished up, then shrugged at her. "Now, how sympathetic do you think the cops will be with me?"

"Wow, you fucked her corpse?" Ashley gasped in horror. "Man, that's just sick."

"Tell me something I *don't* know," Bob miserably agreed. "I'm just glad that I don't remember doing it, or I might very well stick a gun in my mouth."

"Okay, like I really see what you mean now," Ashley said once she'd gotten over her disgust. "Accidentally killing your wife is one thing, but sleeping with her corpse puts you up there in Ed Gein and Jeffrey Dahmer territory."

"Exactly," Bob agreed. "So, what can you do for me? Assuming you can and will help me."

Ashley grinned slightly yellow teeth. "Of course I'll help you, Bob—we're friends, remember? Almost besties, even."

For some reason, the way she said it didn't particularly relax Bob.

"This is gonna cost me . . . how much?" he asked suspiciously.

She waved the question away. "Let's handle one thing at a time—we'll get to payment later."

Bob waited, feeling lost at sea, while for close on five minutes Ashley chewed on her right index fingertip and stared into space like she was thinking hard. Bob spent the time studying her living room and what he could see of the rest of her home.

Ashley had a giant top-of-the-range Samsung home theater system and lots of movie DVDs. Her furniture was also plush and expensive. Seemingly no expense had been spared to make herself comfortable in here.

Hacking and the dark web must pay really well, Bob decided as he squinted, trying to read some close-by movie titles. Most were films he'd never heard of.

He gave up studying her movie collection and returned his attention to her person.

She was still thinking, and he hesitated to break her concentration, but after a few seconds of his staring at her, she blinked several times and then nodded at him.

"Alright, I've worked everything out," she said. "First thing you need to do is dispose of Maryanne's body."

"That's obvious," Bob replied. "That's the reason I'm sitting here in your living room now. I need *you* to help me dispose of Maryanne's body."

But Ashley shook her head. "No, no, you're not thinking straight. Disposing of Maryanne's body is the easy part of things."

"But isn't that what you just said? That I . . . we . . . first need to get rid of her body?"

"Yeah, but not in the sense you're thinking."

"I don't get it."

Ashley frowned. "I'll explain better then. Hiding your wife's corpse is simply the first step in a long process. All that step requires is digging a hole somewhere where she'll never be found, or not found until she's all rotted away and her disappearance can't be connected to you." Then, before Bob could reply to this, Ashley wagged a finger at him. "And let's get this point straight, man—where you put her body is entirely your concern and your responsibility." She got up from the couch and did a pirouette that revealed she might not be wearing any panties beneath her black tee shirt. "I don't do any heavy lifting. It's not that I'm afraid of the cops, but I'm way too delicate for that shit."

Bob nodded. "I imagined you'd have some friends who might . . . you know . . . make the corpse disappear for a price."

Ashley frowned and sat down again. "And whatever gave you that idea about me?" But then she burst out laughing. "Yeah, okay, you're right. I do know a few unsavory characters who could help you bury wifey where she'd never be found."

"Let's call them. Money is no object."

But Ashley shook her head emphatically at him. "No. I like you, Bob, and you don't wanna deal with these guys. They're mobsters, and once they do a job like this for you, they'll bleed you dry for life. One year from now you'll wish you were in jail."

Bob thought hard about that. "Yes, you make a very solid point. But . . . Okay, I'll think of where to bury Maryanne. I'll handle that by myself."

Ashley nodded. "Alright, now we've settled the point that I'm not helping you dig, let's continue with my explanation. I just told you that losing Maryanne where she'll never be found is only the first step in this. Way more important than that is to make her disappearance seem to result from a logical sequence of events that have nothing to do with you."

She paused and stared at him.

"Go on, I'm listening," Bob said, not really understanding. "How are you gonna do that?"

Ashley grinned from ear-to-ear. "By making it appear to everyone, including the police, that the late Maryanne Wilson is still alive and well. So that, when she now suddenly disappears, no one will even start to imagine that her vanishing had anything to do with you."

"You really can do that?"

"Bob, I occasionally perform such duties for the US government; specifically, for the CIA."

CHAPTER 19

Ashley Haskins working for the CIA? Bob had heard stranger things. Despite which, he decided Ashley was just trying to impress him, though he didn't say so to her face.

"Okay, when can we . . . I mean you, get started?" he asked.

"We already have," came the reply. "Now here's what you're going to do."

Bob listened.

"First of all, you're going to tell everyone you know that Maryanne left early and alone for your Acapulco trip."

"How do *you* know about that trip?"

"Simple. Maryanne told my mom, and she told me."

Bob had momentarily forgotten that Maryanne and Jennifer were close friends. "But, won't your mom wonder why Maryanne didn't pop in to say goodbye before she left?"

"Don't worry about that. Leave that to me."

"One other thing that sounds dodgy."

Ashley's lips thinned. "Which is?"

"Ashley, you spoke of leaving a *logical* trail of Maryanne's vanishing. The police will know she didn't get on the plane to Mexico."

But instead of looking daunted by this plot hole, Ashley merely smirked and said, "No, they won't. Once more, just leave it to me." She tapped the couch and said, "Remember what I said. Tell everyone that Ashley left ahead of you for Acapulco. Give anyone who asks the reason that you felt too overworked to travel, and Maryanne insisted on going on ahead alone."

"Okay, I can do that."

Ashley chewed her lip for a little while and then asked: "When's the flight due to depart?"

"Crack of dawn, tomorrow. We're due to be at Logan Airport by 3 a.m. tonight."

"Okay, so you can tell folks tomorrow morning. Or just wait till people start asking why you're still here and she isn't."

"Gotcha."

"I'm gonna need Maryanne's cellphone and her laptop or tablet if she's got one."

"She's got both, but hardly uses her tablet nowadays."

"That's fine, I'll take all three. You do know her passwords, right? To unlock the devices."

"The phone uses thumbprint recognition and her laptop doesn't have a password. I'm not sure about the tablet; she may have set it to recognize her face, but I don't think so."

"Good thing you've not yet gotten buried her body then. Let me put on some shorts and then we'll go down to your place and get her devices. Once I've reset Maryanne's passwords so I can assume her online identity, we'll return up here and discuss my payment."

"Oh, I haven't forgotten about that. Hey, look, how about if *I* go downstairs alone and fetch the things for you? It won't take me more than five minutes, and my going alone also prevents any chance of our being seen together by Amanda and Marvin. And besides, seeing Maryanne in her current state might make you throw up. Dead, she's not the prettiest sight in the world to look at."

"Let's go together. I want to see what wifey looks like before you throw her away for good."

"Ashley, are you always this callous?"

"Look who's talking—the man who killed his wife!"

CHAPTER 20

Allowing Ashley to view Maryanne's body proved much less traumatic than Bob had feared it would be.

Yes, Ashley did at first looked horrified when Bob pulled away the sheet wrapped around the corpse in the bathtub, but after that she behaved in a completely calm and composed manner, placing Maryanne's right thumb against the side of her cellphone to unlock it.

While Ashley worked on the cellphone, Bob studied Maryanne's corpse. He didn't like looking at her face, because her eyes were still rolled up in their sockets, showing just the whites.

"There's something different about her," he told Ashley after a short while of studying the body.

Ashley didn't look away from the cellphone. "What are you talking about?"

"Maryanne's body looks somehow different from the last time I viewed it, which was when I put her in here before heading upstairs to your place."

Ashley still didn't look away from Maryanne's cellphone. Now she seemed to be taking her picture with it. "She's just begun decaying, that's all."

But Bob didn't believe that was all that was wrong with Maryanne's body. Bob didn't think corpses decayed that fast, and anyway, the oddity he felt he was noticing wasn't rotting flesh. But he couldn't pinpoint the difference.

Nah, you're just seeing things, he decided after a while. *A corpse doesn't alter after its creation.*

"Alright, we're done here," Ashley finally said. "I've successfully set your wife's phone to recognize my own thumbprint and face instead." She gestured dismissively at the corpse. "You can cover her up again."

This Bob quickly did. Before entering the bathroom, the two of them had already confirmed that they wouldn't need passwords for either Maryanne's laptop or tablet.

Bob locked the bathroom, but left the key in the lock.

53

"Okay," Ashley said, jerking her head towards the living room. "Let's go back up to my place and talk business."

Bob followed meekly, now feeling like a lamb being led to the slaughter.

What will the butcher's knife feel like on my neck? he wondered.

CHAPTER 21

"So, what will your help cost me?" Bob asked Ashley, when they were once more seated in her living room. "I don't have a lot of money, but you can have all of it, and more too, once I get it. I just got promoted at work and that's a huge hike in my salary."

But Ashley smiled. "I don't want your money." She gestured around her home. "I make enough online to pay my bills and afford those luxuries I want. And I'm not greedy. So, I won't attempt to bleed you dry."

Bob nodded, his mouth suddenly dry. "Okay, so what do you want from me in return for your help?"

"I want you to be my boyfriend, that's all. Yes, or no?"

"What?" Bob said this simply to buy time. Now that they were conspirators, now that Ashley Haskins had become an accessory to Maryanne's death, Bob had already sensed a subtle shift in their relationship. On their way back here, Ashley had slipped her arm through his while they'd climbed the steps, and was now sitting closer to him on the couch than she had before. And while replying him just now, she'd moved even closer still, until now their legs were touching.

"I said, I want you to be my boyfriend," Ashley repeated. "I've had my heart set on you from the first moment I saw you. But of course, you were faithful to your wife. But now that you're a widower . . ."

Bob winced at the word 'widower.' But at least it sounded better than 'murderer.' *Just this morning I was happily married to the woman of my dreams. It's not evening yet and I'm single again and being propositioned by a woman whom I've spent the past year avoiding.*

"Hey, what about Tony?" he asked. "He isn't going to like me breaking up your relationship."

Ashley's expression turned bitter. "Fuck Tony. The asshole's been sleeping with other women behind my back. Good riddance to his cheating ass."

Bob felt sympathetic to Ashley when she said this. After all, his current problem was caused by a cheating spouse. But then he realized that Ashley's voice pleaded for no sympathy. She sounded as if Tony was already dead to her.

"This is kinda sudden, don't you think?" Bob said. "Can I have some time to think about it?"

"We're having a business discussion, not a romantic one," was Ashley's reply. "You want something from me, and in return I want something from you. And be warned, Bob, your being my boyfriend is the *only* condition under which I'll keep you out of jail."

Bob forced a smile. "Okay, we have a deal."

"Oh, not so fast—there's more," Ashley said.

"More? What else can there possibly be? You asked me to be your man, and I agreed."

"I'm a sadist. You'll have to be my slave too."

Bob's mouth twisted up. He'd never been one for kinky sex. "You're telling me you're a dominatrix? You want to tie me up?"

But she shook her head. "No, not a dominatrix. A *sadist*. That means I like to hurt people. Hurting people turns me on. It's how I get my sexual satisfaction."

"Oh. And you're proposing to hurt me to get your satisfaction?"

She smiled a cruel smile. "Exactly. So, before you accept to be my boyfriend you might want to consider things very carefully. If you do agree to date me, I'll take care of things for you so wonderfully that it'll be like Maryanne never existed. But in return, you'll have to satisfy my own desires, no matter how twisted they may seem to you, no matter how painful at times."

"Hmmm. How long will this painful relationship go on for?"

"At least three years; more if you want it to. I'm figuring that even on a manslaughter charge, that's the least prison time you'll do."

Bob thought about it for a while. He really did. *Nothing's free. Nothing's easy. I'm screwed either way. But better to be screwed outside the penitentiary than to be taking it up the ass every night and have other guys calling me 'darling.' Starting a new relationship on the same day that my wife died is just nasty, but I really don't have any choice in the matter. Fuck or be fucked is the law of the jungle here.*

"Okay," he said slowly. "I agree. I'll be your boyfriend."

"And my *slave*," Ashley added with a feverish look on her face, and a strange glow in her eyes. "You must agree to that condition also. You must agree that you'll be my slave."

"Hasn't slavery been abolished here in the USA?"

"Don't joke about this. Being my boyfriend includes being my slave. I can't have one without the other." She grimaced. "Which is why my relationship with that asshole Tony turned sour. He couldn't stand my heat and so fled my kitchen."

Bob nodded. "Okay, lady. Get me out of the legal frying pan and I'll jump in your S and M fire. Yeah, I'll be your slave too."

"Your wish is my command," Ashley said, looking like a child at Christmas who'd gotten all the presents she'd ever wanted in her short life. Ashley leaned forward and kissed him on the lips and then got up off of the couch and walked off toward her kitchen.

"Relax, darling," she called back to him. "I'll pour us a couple of drinks to celebrate the beginning of our loving relationship."

She was back in a few minutes with two glasses of wine and a tray of sandwiches. "Eat up, honey," she said cheerfully. "You'll need all the energy you can muster to dig a deep grave for Maryanne."

CHAPTER 22

For the second time today, Bob suddenly snapped awake. For the second time today, Bob realized that his slumber had been caused by alcohol. For the second time today, Bob realized that he'd woken up in a different location than that in which he'd fallen asleep. And for the second time today, Bob discovered that he'd woken up naked.

This time it took Bob much longer to wrap his mind around his waking circumstances. And even then, understanding those circumstances required his remembering in detail his conversation with Ashley before slumber came.

Oh no. Oh, hell no! Oh no! Ashley didn't!

Bob was now a captive.

He'd woken up standing upright, prevented from falling because he was bound to an X-frame in a mostly empty room. The frame was a sturdy metal one that was fitted with different sorts of restraints. Trying to get free convinced Bob that he was firmly bound in place.

There was a gag-ball in his mouth. He tried to spit out the perforated rubber barrier, but without success.

Arranged in ranks on the wall opposite him were any number of whips and floggers; some made of leather, some of metal, some of plastic; some that were even peeled tree branches. There were also riding crops of different sizes and colorations.

But this selection of whips and floggers was merely the tip of the sadistic iceberg, as a look around the room quicky revealed. All four of this room's walls were hung with instruments of torture, some of which Bob recognized from books or movies or the internet, and good number that he didn't.

Frighteningly, there were many knives on the walls also, both hung in racks and singly, and shelves of hammers and other implements of torment. There were also leather and latex masks in various styles and colors.

Also prominent and evident were the video cameras. Bob counted four of these modern digital units. Three of the cameras were fixed on tripods and angled so they faced him, and a fourth, smaller camera lay on one of the three padded couches in the room

Ashley obviously likes filming her fun too. What the hell was I thinking when I agreed to this?

The room felt strange and it stank of body fluids; sweat, urine, and feces; and maybe even dried blood, though Bob refused to dwell on this last possibility.

There was a second X-frame beside the one to which Bob was chained, and from the top of which dangled several wires that ended in gleaming crocodile clips and were likely connected to batteries out of sight.

Bob understood that he was chained in a torture chamber. His new girlfriend's—Ashley's—torture chamber. This room had to be a bedroom in her condo.

I was right to think there was something wrong about her. I can't even begin to figure out how long it took her to collect all of this crazy stuff in here, or how much money it cost her to buy it all, or . . . how many people she's hurt within these four walls.

And apparently, he would be next.

I need to yell for help! I need to get out of here! he thought desperately. But Ashley had clearly drugged the wine she'd given him. Now that he was awake, Bob barely had the strength to remain upright. Even if Ashley had chained him less securely, he wasn't about going anywhere.

CHAPTER 23

The door opened, and Ashley walked in.

Behind her, before she shut the door, a slice of her living room was visible at the end of the hallway. So, he'd been right. He was still in her condo. He wondered in amazement how neither he nor Maryanne had ever suspected just how twisted their youngest upstairs neighbor was.

"Hmmph, hmmph!" Bob growled against the gagball, which tasted bitter and made him wonder how many other mouths it had been in before his, and if those mouths had been clean or dirty, or even diseased. It was a disgusting thread of contemplation.

Ashley walked over to stand in front of him. She was naked except for a pair of red high heels and red lace panties. Her breasts were large and sagged a little. Her naked body was sexually alluring and began to give him an erection, but the thoughts of what she intended to do to him in here quickly killed his arousal.

He could only stare at her in horror as she turned away from him and began to study the whips arrayed on the wall facing him.

"Don't worry, Bob," Ashley said over her shoulder as her fingers trailed from whip to whip, occasionally stopping to fondle one or other of them lovingly, like she remembered something special about it. "I'm not going to kill you or do anything that will permanently damage you in any way, except maybe psychologically." She laughed and pulled a long black whip off the wall, a whip that seemed to be almost six feet long.

"Oh no, I'm not going to kill you, baby," she told Bob with a mean gleam in her eye. "Although there'll definitely be times during our relationship when you'll wish that I simply would."

And then the whipping began. It was utter total torment, like Bob imagined the torments of hell must be like. Bob had never experienced such pain in his life before, nor had he imagined such pain existed. Each crack of Ashley's whip against his flesh seemed to be cutting him into little pieces, as if each resulting welt went deeper than the skin it left red and in places even bleeding.

"Take this, darling! And this! And this!" Ashley said, with a broad smile, her eyes bright, her face flushed with lust, the voice in which she harangued him little more than a throaty croak. When Bob managed to concentrate through the pain he was suffering, he saw that Ashley's nipples were hard. Occasionally, when her whip arm grew tired, she paused and dug her free hand in her panties and rubbed her sex.

After the first few slashes of the whip Bob was glad the gag-ball was in his mouth. Without its restraint on his voice, he'd have been screaming like a baby.

The fact that Ashley was video-recording everything made everything that much worse. She would watch this later and relive her pleasure and his pain over and over again.

Ashley whipped him methodically, first the front of his body and then the back, down to his thighs and feet, and then up again to his torso. She spared no area of his body except his face and head, the arms raised beside them, and his penis and testicles. But the lashing she gave his bared buttocks seemed to more than compensate for her sparing his genitals.

He felt no erotic stimulation, just consistent and unceasing pain.

Ashley, however, was clearly rising to the heights of sexual ecstasy. For the past two or three minutes, she'd whipped him ceaselessly, with her left hand stuck deep in her panties, rubbing herself for all she was worth. This of course reduced the force with which she cracked the whip at him, but by then Bob was already in such agony that this reduction hardly counted for anything.

Then all of a sudden, when Bob was losing his mind from the pain of the ceaseless lashing, Ashley froze like a statue and orgasmed.

"Fuck, yes, yes, yes!" she gasped, trembling in place with her legs pressed tightly together and her face now assuming a transcendent rapturous expression.

Then her sexual crisis passed and she ran forward and grabbed Bob, pressing her body tightly against his and kissing his gagged lips, while gasping: "Oh, Bob, I love you so much. I just love you so much, darling!"

Bob of course, couldn't reply. *If this is your definition of love, I'll take hatred any day,* he thought.

Then Ashley knelt down, took his cock in her mouth and began sucking on him. Bob didn't understand how he could possibly get an erection with the way he was currently hurting, but when, after a while of Ashley's fellating him and playing with his testicles, he did grow erect, he figured it was simply his body's way of seeking release from the torment it was in.

Ashley sucked on him delicately until he ejaculated into her mouth, a sexual release of mingled ecstasy and agony.

Ashley then straightened up and hugged him again.

"Oh, man, I just love you so much!" she gasped against his hurting flesh, with his semen dribbling from her mouth onto his belly.

This time Bob didn't hear her words of endearment. He'd passed out from the sensation overload.

CHAPTER 24

Bob had no idea when he revived again. But by then he was no longer chained to Ashley's whipping frame. Instead, he was lying in a soft and very comfortable bed.

He looked around Ashley's bedroom, but saw no sign of her, his terrifying tormentor.

He still hurt, but oddly enough, even though his skin was crisscrossed with bright red welts, his wounds no longer stung as much as they had during his whipping. Touching his skin soon provided an answer for this. His skin felt moist in an unfamiliar way, which Bob took to mean that Ashley had rubbed an anesthetic cream over his welts while he slept. While he appreciated her doing so, her consideration of him in this area hardly served to lessen his newly-discovered dread of her.

The woman is simply nuts. No wonder Tony fled from her.

The bed in which he lay was oh, so comforting. And seeing as he was at the tail end of a long period of overwork, Bob felt like just lying in here and sleeping.

But two things galvanized him into motion. First of all, he didn't like the idea of leaving Maryanne's corpse downstairs all alone in their condo. However illogical this line of reasoning may be, leaving his dead wife's body unattended tonight struck Bob as wrong. And secondly, Bob had no idea what Ashley might desire of him when she came to bed. What if she was a sadist nymphomaniac and had only patched him up so she could cause him more pain?

Bob knew he had no tolerance for any more pain tonight. He got out of her bed and looked around for his clothes.

Ashley had hung his clothes inside her closet. There were also other male clothes in there that had to belong to her ex-boyfriend Tony.

Bob dressed quickly, worried that at any minute he might hear Ashley opening the bedroom door, and she might prevent him from leaving. But it didn't happen.

Unable to find his shoes in her bedroom, he slipped out into the dimly lit hallway, and headed for her living room.

While making his escape, Bob discovered why Ashley hadn't yet come to bed. She was hunched over a laptop in another room along the hallway, this one a shrine to electronic devices, full of glowing screens and flashing LEDs and illuminated keyboards. Light from this workroom spilled out into the hallway in a starry rectangular configuration.

He didn't wait to see clearly what she was doing, but she seemed locked in concentration.

He stepped quietly past her and entered the living room. There he gathered up his shoes from near the couch, retrieved his cellphone from an end table, opened up Ashley's front door without putting his shoes on, and after a final nervous glance back down the hallway, stepped out into the third-floor corridor and clicked the door shut behind him.

He felt like he'd just escaped from prison.

CHAPTER 25

Once back in his own condo, Bob went straight through to his kitchen and brewed himself an extra-strong mug of coffee.

Now that he'd left Ashley's condo, the psychic cushion he'd had of things being under control no longer soothed him. The need to bury Maryanne's body rang warning bells in his head. He felt overcome by a sense of urgency. He tried to rationally disperse this sense of urgency.

Fuck it—I'll do it tomorrow night. Too much has happened today for me to properly concentrate on such a gruesome task, which is going to require me being at my mental peak. And besides, I don't even have any idea where exactly to bury Maryanne. He grimaced at the tingling of the welts on his skin, a sensation like ghosts were dancing in lines across his body. *And last of all, I just got whipped like a dog, and once Ashley's anesthetic wears off, I'll be hurting like hell.*

But he knew he was simply deceiving himself. He needed to inter Maryanne's remains tonight.

But where exactly? And what happens if, after I cut her up—because I don't see how I'll ever carry a woman-shaped package out to my truck with no one in the building noticing me doing it—what if after cutting Maryanne in pieces, I'm driving along with my dead wife's remains in the back of my pickup truck and the State Police pull me over? Once they find her chopped-up body . . .

The rest didn't even bear considering. No matter how good Ashley's digital witchery was, Bob would be guesting in a stone motel for the next century at least.

The more I think about this, the more it seems I'll be better off simply coming clean to the police, and taking my chances with them.

While he was considering this, his cellphone rang. He looked at the screen. It was Ashley calling. He considered not answering; and then considered that this was as good a time as any to end their relationship.

"Hello, darling," she said in a creamy voice. "You left without saying goodnight."

"Yeah, I know. Listen, Ashley, I'm sorry, but I can't hack this sort of sadistic relationship. If you whip me one more time like that, I'm gonna die."

"But we had a deal," she said, with some anger in her voice. "I take care of you and you—"

"Sooner or later, you'll kill me anyway. I saw all the stuff you've got in that torture chamber of yours."

Now she laughed. "Oh, most of it's just for show. I never cut anyone, for instance—I'm not really into that 'blood play' stuff. Except you want us to try it."

Bob saw nothing funny about it. "Listen. Thanks, but no thanks. I think I'll rather take my chances with the police. I'll turn myself in in the morning. At least they won't whip me."

Now Ashley didn't laugh. "You're being premature. Before you do anything stupid, check your Facebook updates. That's what I just called to tell you about."

"What the hell are you talking about?"

"You've got a cellphone like I have. Check your damn Facebook updates, darling."

She hung up. After staring at his phone in confusion for while, Bob checked his recent Facebook notifications.

He almost immediately noted that he had several from 'Maryanne Wilson.' More bemused than curious, he clicked on one to see what it contained. And then he spent the next five minutes replaying the video clip of Maryanne at Boston's Logan Airport, taking a selfie, saying "Bye, bye USA," and then waving at the camera. The woman in the video was his dead wife, no doubt about it.

The video itself had been posted last night at 10:30 p.m. The time was now 1:47 a.m.

Now very curious and interested, Bob checked his other Facebook notifications that related to Maryanne's trip south. All of these either involved her taking video selfies at the airport, or updating her Facebook status. One of Maryanne's selfies even showed her having her luggage checked by Customs officials.

But something now struck Bob as wrong.

Hey, hey, now wait a minute. Our flight to Mexico was supposed to leave at 5:30 tomorrow morning. So, what the hell is this? Why has Ashley put Maryanne at Logan Airport tonight?

Then he noticed something else that was strange: Maryanne supposedly wasn't heading to Mexico anymore, but would be traveling further south, to Maiquetía in Venezuela.

Despite being perplexed by this disparity of detail, Bob was very impressed by what he was viewing. This level of video fakery seemed like sorcery to him. How the hell had Ashley Haskins placed Maryanne at Logan Airport in Boston tonight, when she was actually lying dead in the guest bathroom?

Damn, she's good! I suppose if she can do this, I can endure a little pain!

He decided to call Ashley back and let her know their deal was still on.

But his phone was already ringing again, and once again it was Ashley calling him.

"So, what do you think, darling?" she asked once he'd picked up. "Am I holding up my end of our bargain, or what?" Bob noticed that she sounded a little worried, as if unsure he wouldn't still go through with his plan to turn himself in to the police in the morning. She sounded almost desperate that he not surrender himself to the law.

He decided to set her mind at ease. "Okay, baby, I've reconsidered my options. We've still got a deal."

"Really? You won't wuss out on me again?"

"Really. How the hell did you make those videos?"

"Deep-fake stuff. The sort of thing I occasionally do for our government."

"Yeah, yeah. But why did you switch her destination from Acapulco to . . . where was it again?"

"Don't worry about it. Just trust me. All will be revealed in due time."

There was a pause and then Ashley asked: "Bob, how far have you gotten with burying Maryanne's body? It'll be best to do it tonight."

"I'm having a huge problem with that," Bob explained. "I don't know where to bury her."

"You could try the Pleasant Street Cemetery," was Ashley's immediate reply. "I was gonna suggest that if you'd told me when you were leaving here. That's a great place to bury her."

Bob almost yelled his reply into the phone. "Are you trying to get me busted? That's right beside the police station!"

"Hey, calm down. It was just a girlfriendly suggestion. But I'm not joking. The cops never go there; and consider this: who'll ever think of looking for a corpse in a graveyard? The police never search for murder victims in the cemetery. Just go to the Pleasant Street Cemetery with a shovel and bury her down by the north side, where there's a whole forest of trees. There aren't many houses out there, so no one's gonna see you do it. But bury her real deep; you don't want the dogs smelling her down there and dragging her up to the surface. But otherwise, you can rest assured she won't be found for years and years."

Bob nodded at the cellphone.

"Oh, and one more thing," Ashley added. "Whatever the hell else you do, don't bury Maryanne anywhere near Brian Chu's grave."

"Who's Brian Chu?"

"I'm not sure myself, but everyone I know says the guy's grave is bad juju. Real bad juju. In addition to the tombstone, his grave has got its own metal picket fence under the trees, so you can't miss it."

"Okay," Bob said. "That's exactly where I'll go and bury Maryanne. I'm going to have to cut her up though, so I'd better get off of the phone and get started on that."

"Cut her up? Well, do so if you think it's necessary."

"I think it is. I really don't want to butcher Maryanne, but I don't see any other way to handle it. Ashley, you saw her—she's stuck in rigor mortis; she's so stiff now, it'll be impossible to get her out of the house unnoticed otherwise."

"Okay, but please be very careful that you don't get caught. I don't want you getting into any trouble." Ashley blew him a kiss over the phone. "Call me in the morning and let me know how it goes, okay? And we'll see each other again tomorrow night."

"It's a date," Bob said. "Hey, can I get some more of that salve you rubbed on me?"

"Yeah, sure. I'll leave a jar of it by your door on my way out in the morning. Goodnight, baby."

"Goodnight, darling."

Bob hung up and stared at his cellphone in disgust.

Yesterday morning I didn't even like this woman and now we're supposedly in love. Wow, crime makes for really strange bedfellows.

Then he went into the kitchen to both find a cleaver to chop Maryanne up with, and some garbage bags to store her remains in.

CHAPTER 26

Once Bob had armed himself with the largest meat cleaver he could find in the house, he returned to the bathroom.

His plan was to cut Maryanne apart in the bathtub, where all the blood could drain away and he'd not need to mop the floor too much afterwards.

On opening the bathroom door, Bob noted that although most of the air freshener he'd earlier sprayed in there had now dispersed, there was still no reek of putrefaction.

But immediately Bob pulled back the sheet he'd wrapped Maryanne up in, he saw that something was now glaringly different about her body.

Maryanne was now a bright blue in color. As blue as the sky on a bright summer day. Bob had no idea what to make of this. Just to make certain of what he was seeing, he yanked the sheet completely off of her.

Yes, she was blue all over as she lay on her back in the bathtub. Even between her legs, she had a blue tunnel instead of the previous pink one. The only things about her that had remained the same were her blonde hair (both on her head and in her pubic region) and the whites of her eyes, which had now turned a sickly yellow.

Bob stepped back from the corpse and regarded it in a state of confusion.

What the hell?

The only possible cause Bob could come up with for his dead wife's blue transformation was tissue decay. But she clearly wasn't decaying. In fact, even up close like this, her body hardly smelt at all.

Was this what I noticed earlier while I was in here with Ashley? No, I don't think so. What do I do now? Do I call Ashley and tell her about this? There's no point in my doing that. She won't know what to make of this either. I'd better just continue with the original plan of cutting Maryanne into smaller pieces.

As additionally unpleasant as the task of cutting up Maryanne had now become—because, what if her current blue state was the result of an infection she'd contracted from her adulterous lover?—Bob decided to get on with it.

The garbage bags are waiting and Maryanne certainly isn't going to obligingly fall apart by herself.

So, after placing the garbage bags on the floor and the cleaver in the washstand, Bob grabbed hold of Maryanne's right arm to position her body better.

But the moment he touched her blue skin, something hit him. What Bob felt wasn't physical, but an intense wave of mental repulsion that immediately made him let go of her again.

Bob shook his head and decided he'd just imagined it. There was no one in here except himself and the body. He had to be spooking himself, projecting his own distaste at the corpse.

So, he grabbed hold of Maryanne's body again. The intense sense of repulsion immediately hit him again, much stronger this time.

Bob refused to let go of Maryanne, however. He'd begun straightening her out in the tub, when a force—it felt as if someone had swatted him away—a force knocked him away from Maryanne and slammed him against the bathroom wall, right next to the open door.

Bob fell to the ground and sat there for a moment, looking and feeling stunned. He was too confused to be frightened. He had no idea what to make of what had just happened.

And before he could form an opinion, things got even stranger. Maryanne's sky-blue corpse began moving. First her stiff limbs began jerking, and then after a few seconds, she slowly got up to her feet, standing up in the bathtub.

Bob watched in disbelief. He felt like fleeing in terror, but didn't, partly because he thought he was dreaming; and where could one run from a dream?

But this was clearly no dream.

Maryanne clearly wasn't alive either. Although she was now standing upright, her head wasn't; it still lolled crazily sideways on her shattered neck vertebrae. Also, her now-yellow eyes were still rolled up into their sockets.

She stood there, looking like an evil puppet hanging on invisible strings. The sight of her filled Bob with terror; whatever courage he'd earlier felt now fled from him.

The bathroom door was right beside Bob, wide open in fact, but it seemed a million miles away. If Maryanne were to take a single step in Bob's direction now, if she stepped out of the bathtub, he felt he'd go stark raving mad.

But she didn't move from where she stood. Instead, Bob suddenly heard a voice speaking.

"Hunger . . . hungry . . . food . . . food," the voice said.

The voice was low and guttural and was clearly coming from Maryanne, but her lips weren't moving, so Bob knew he was hearing it in his head. However, even though it was definitely coming from the reanimated corpse a few yards away, what Bob was hearing wasn't Maryanne's voice. Bob had no idea whose voice it was.

"Food . . . must eat . . . raw meat . . . meat . . ."

The voice kept on speaking in this vein, an insistent throbbing pulse like a migraine that as much forced Bob to his feet as did the realization that if he didn't do something about Maryanne's request, she might just eat him instead, though she still wasn't moving from where she stood inside the bathtub.

So, trembling with fright, Bob leapt up and ran out of the bathroom. He ran to the kitchen, and opening up the freezer compartment of their fridge, pulled out four large steaks.

"Food . . . food . . . feed me!" The demonic voice pounded in his head.

Bob ran back to the bathroom. Not daring to go close to Maryanne now, he flung the steaks into the bathtub instead.

He stood there in the doorway, shivering, wondering why he'd not simply fled out of the house instead of going to the kitchen; wondering why afterwards he'd even come back here; and wondering how in the hell, with her neck broken and her head hanging awkwardly like that, Maryanne was going to eat the raw meat he'd just thrown to her.

His third question was quickly answered.

"Yes . . . FOOOD!" the voice in his head enthused, as Maryanne squatted down in the bathtub over the steaks.

Then in a gush of wetness, an arm spurted out of her vagina. The arm was blue in color, and, except for the hand at its end, could easily have been mistaken for a worm emerging from Maryanne's body. Feeling nauseated, Bob watched the hand at the end of the arm scoop up the steaks, and then drag them back up into Maryanne's body.

The voice/urgency in Bob's head now faded away, leaving behind a sense of deep satisfaction.

Bob managed not to throw up as the lips of Maryanne's sex closed over the slimy hand again. But he couldn't watch anymore.

It was also glaringly obvious to him now that he wouldn't be disposing of Maryanne's corpse tonight.

So, foreseeing no use for them anymore, as Maryanne got back up to her feet again, Bob retrieved the garbage bags from the bathroom floor, picked up the meat cleaver from the washstand sink and then got out of there.

Bob shut the bathroom door and locked it.

He returned to the kitchen, put both cleaver and black bags away again, and washed his hands. Then realizing he was still trembling from what he'd just experienced, he retrieved the bottle of Wild Turkey from where he'd earlier replaced it, and poured himself a tall glass of bourbon whiskey. He carried the glass outside into the living room, and sat down. Staring at the hallway entrance, he attempted to make sense of what had just happened.

She's alive! No, she's dead! No, Maryanne's not dead . . . she's . . . yes, she's dead! But . . .

He was too confused and scared to do anything but continue to be confused and scared. He stared at the front door, wondering if he could simply run away from it all. But he felt trapped. There seemed no salvation outside of his house.

Call Ashley? She'll just think I'm nuts. She'll think I'm trying to chicken out of disposing of Maryanne's corpse. Well, at least I've fed the blue thing, whatever she or rather 'it' is now. It should be okay till morning.

It had been a long and crazy twenty-four hours for Bob Wilson. First, he'd killed his wife, then he'd been whipped by his new sadist girlfriend . . . and now his dead wife seemed to have returned from the dead to haunt him.

Bob decided 'fuck it all.' He finished up his whiskey, turned off the house lights and went to bed.

He fell asleep almost immediately.

CHAPTER 27

Bob awoke very late on Friday morning, having slept almost till noon.

The sun was shining and somewhere nearby a bird was singing. It seemed a lovely day. But then he reached sideways in the bed, felt for Maryanne, and all of yesterday's happenings came back to his mind.

His body ached from its webbing of welts. When he shifted on the sheets, it felt like he was lying on a bed of razor blades. Because his arms had been secured above his head, they had been spared the lash. Which was good, as it meant that so long as he wore pants, he'd be spared the embarrassment of explaining why he was all striped up like a zebra.

Frowning and now feeling the start of a hangover, he got out of bed and went to brush his teeth.

He took his time with getting cleaned up. For the moment there seemed no urgency; he was on vacation now and could take his time. No more needing to dash out the door at 6 a.m. with just coffee in his belly, to cover for someone else's screwups.

And besides, for the time being at least, yesterday's events had the element of a dream to them. No one's life could get so messed up in less than twenty-four hours. It seemed that way to Bob Wilson; that he was merely the pawn in a massive cosmic joke. He was simply catching the spillover of someone else's vivid nightmare.

There's no blue monster in the guest bathroom . . . Oh, dude, but yes, there is.

Staring morosely at the swollen red lines on his body, Bob remembered that Ashley had said she'd drop off the bottle of salve at his doorstep. He went through the living room to the front door, opened it up and looked. No salve.

Meaning Ashley is undoubtedly still asleep. I'd better go and look at . . .

But he didn't feel like facing the blue version of his late wife yet. He wasn't worried about feeding her/it—there were still steaks in the freezer—but he liked this halcyon 'calm before the storm' period. Once he looked in on the monster, he'd have to think of what to do about it. Until he opened that bathroom door, however, he could still

73

imagine that Maryanne would be as dead in there as she'd been earlier last night.

Not that that was really much better; but at least it could be explained.

Still postponing the inevitable, Bob stepped out onto his balcony.

Almost immediately, he spotted Jennifer wheeling her husband Chris over to their car, most likely taking Chris for an appointment with his doctor. Ashley wasn't with them, which would've been odd if Bob didn't know that she was still asleep. Ashley usually helped her mother with getting her father in and out of their car.

As Jennifer single-handedly moved Chris into the front seat of their blue Nissan, Bob remembered an erotic dream he'd had about her a week ago. He and Jennifer had been somewhere making love, doing it in all sorts of sexual positions. It had been an enjoyable dream, but one he'd instantly forgotten because of how overworked he was at the time.

Musing on it now, he smiled. Not that he'd ever hit on Jennifer, but she did look nice for her age.

Oh, how I wish everything going on now really is a dream, he thought, as he turned away from the balcony and went to look in on his pet monster.

CHAPTER 28

When Bob opened the bathroom door, he found Maryanne's corpse pacing about in there. The blue corpse was out of the bathtub now and was walking back and forth through the bathroom in an aimless sort of way, pacing till it hit one wall, then altering direction and pacing until it struck another wall. Most times the first part of Maryanne's body to hit the wall was her dangling head, which then snapped back as if her neck was being broken all over again.

The sight was horrible to behold.

Bob stared at the pacing corpse for a while before she seemed to notice him.

"Food . . . food!" she grunted in his head.

Bob tossed the blue female corpse the three steaks that he'd brought with him, and watched her squat down and perform the same nauseating process of eating them through her vagina, from which this time, *two* blue arms emerged to retrieve the food.

Guttural feeding noises echoed in Bob's head.

Bob winced as shreds of meat dropped from Maryanne's crotch to the bathroom floor.

That was bad enough to view. But even worse, once Bob had gotten over his revulsion at the corpse's feeding process, was his realization that something else had altered about her.

Maryanne was now visibly pregnant. Her body had markedly thickened around her midriff like all pregnancies did after a while.

Bob tried to make sense of what he was seeing. He'd have liked to conclude that it was the food making her bulge out like this, but he knew that wasn't the case.

Those two blue arms that come out of her body to pick up the food I throw to her, they must belong to the baby in her womb. And it's growing, apparently by the hour. The 'baby' is what's keeping Maryanne's body alive, and that baby is what's talking to me. But . . . what the hell sort of a baby can possibly keep growing inside a dead woman? And why does it have a blue body? Did she have an affair with a demon!?

75

Seemingly content with the food 'she' had consumed, 'Maryanne' got up from the floor and resumed her aimless pacing through the bathroom.

After getting out of her way once, when she walked straight and unseeing directly at him, Bob stepped outside the bathroom again and locked it up tight.

He remembered the gun in his nightstand, and wondered if, now that Jennifer and Chris were both out of the house, he should try to use it on the unborn creature. But thoughts of shooting Maryanne, even in her current postmortem messed-up state, simply upset him further.

Bob felt more confused than ever. Finally, after sitting undecided in his living room for a while, he got up and fetched his cellphone and car keys from the bedroom.

The time now was almost 2 p.m. Bob realized he hadn't even looked at his phone today, a testimony to just how distracted he'd been since waking up.

Now, he checked his phone messages and he saw that 'Maryanne' had safely arrived in Maiquetía, Venezuela, and had just posted a selfie of herself at Simón Bolívar Airport. He read the comments under her post. Two of her friends had already asked "Where's Bob?" to which Maryanne had replied. "Oh, Bob is doing what he's got to do, while I'm doing what I've gotta do."

One friend had commented on that: "I thought you were both traveling together to Mexico."

To which 'Maryanne' had replied: "That was then, this is now! #NewMe #NoMoreChains."

Maryanne's reply seemed to Bob an odd one for a happily married woman to make, and he determined to discuss it with Ashley when he visited her place tonight.

Ashley hadn't yet called him, or even sent him a message to enquire how his trip to bury Maryanne had worked out. Remembering how Jennifer had single-handedly had to lift Chris into their car, Bob figured that Ashley must have worked through the night and only gotten to bed in the dawn hours.

He went downstairs, started up his car and drove out of the parking lot.

He had no idea exactly where he was driving to, but he'd decided he needed to get out of the house for a while today.

Bob needed to leave all the horror behind him, if only for a few hours.

CHAPTER 29

Bob spent most of the afternoon doing nothing. Then, as the sun was setting, he drove to a grocery store and bought fifty pounds of raw meat, telling the checkout cashier that he was planning on hosting a barbeque over the weekend.

He loaded the meat up into his pickup truck and drove on back home.

By the tally of cars in the parking lot, Jennifer and Chris were back from the hospital, Ashley was home, Rodney was out, and both Amanda and Marvin were home; this last being clear because Marvin's black and silver Harley was parked next to Amanda's black BMW.

Bob got out of his pickup truck and grimaced up at the darkened windows of his condo unit. Brief as the respite may have been, being away from home today had done him a load of good. For a few hours he'd been able to simply forget his personal crisis. He'd driven down to neighboring Taunton and had a hearty lunch at a Mexican restaurant, after which he'd driven to a nearby park and fallen asleep on a park bench, only waking up when it began raining. Even the welts from yesterday's lashing hadn't bothered him much.

But now I'm back home, and I need to face the beast in the bathroom again. Shit!

By the time he'd carried his bags of raw meat from the elevator to his front door, all the mental benefits of the past few hours of relaxation seemed to have left him. When he stepped through his front door, he once more felt haggard, stressed beyond belief, and tired out.

Bob packed most of the purchased meat into his fridge. Then he picked up the chunks of flesh he'd saved for Maryanne's demon fetus and went to feed it.

In the bathroom, nothing had changed. Maryanne's blue body was still pacing back and forth and bumping into wall after wall, on one occasion even falling into the bathtub, and then climbing out of there only to walk belly-first into the washing machine. Her pregnancy seemed about the same size as it had been in the morning.

Bob flung the meat at the corpse and got out of there before he had to witness her obscene feeding process again.

Then he tried to relax. As great as being away from the house all day had been, he'd not been able to come up with a solution to the 'blue-skinned thing' in the bathroom. Maybe discussing it with Ashley would help. He had to anyway; she was now as much a part of things as he was.

Outside of the condo, the night was dark. Time for his date with Ashley. He winced at the memory of last night's brutal lashing and hoped she didn't intend more of the same for him.

CHAPTER 30

Ashley was visibly delighted to see Bob. Grabbing hold of his arm, she hurriedly led him to her large living room couch and seated him. She had a tray set on the coffee table, with sandwiches and a bottle of wine.

She'd clearly been expecting him, possibly even counting the minutes till he arrived at her condo. Bob knew this because she'd taken extra care with her appearance, even putting on some makeup. She was wearing a flimsy nightgown that parted in the middle, revealing she had nothing on underneath.

Bob initially ignored her seductiveness.

"Honey, we've got a problem," he began saying, but either he'd not spoken loudly enough or Ashley was so wrapped up in her delight at seeing him that she wasn't paying any attention to what he was saying. Or maybe, she simply pretended not to hear him, because she didn't feel like dealing with anything serious at the moment.

Whatever her reason, ignoring his statement, she turned away from him and began pouring out wine into their glasses.

Bob watched her with suspicion. He feared that that the wine was drugged, like he suspected yesterday's wine had been too. He decided he wouldn't have any wine unless Ashley drank some first.

I've no idea how I fell asleep in here yesterday night; and I don't want a sequel.

Bob was suddenly struck by the realization that Ashley Haskins was clearly a very smart cookie. From the way she'd so far made no comments about his lack of IT savvy (glaringly demonstrated by his uneducated questions about her work on his behalf), he figured she'd already deduced that she'd been mistaken about the exact nature of his professional qualifications. This was a relief of sorts to Bob, as it meant he needn't pretend an understanding of things that at work he generally left to the digital wizards.

Ashley looked up from filling their glasses.

"So, baby, you know what time of the night it is, don't'cha?" she said. "Oh, yeah, it's S and M time!"

That statement so upset and worried Bob Wilson that he was suddenly unable to think of anything else. Deciding it would be best to get things over with as quickly as possible, he'd been about to tell Ashley about the living-dead woman in his living quarters, intending to make her listen despite her haze of lust.

But on hearing the dreaded words 'S and M,' Bob's tongue froze in his mouth. His tale of inexplicable terror locked up in his throat, paralyzed into nonexistence by the very real threat of physical agony that those two dreaded letters summoned to his mind. The entire developing living-dead woman crisis downstairs paled into total insignificance when rated alongside of Bob's desire to avoid a similar torment to yesterday's.

"Hell no!" he protested. "So soon? You can't be serious."

But Ashley's response was to hug and kiss him, and to rub her breasts against him.

Then she sat on his thighs and tilted a wineglass to his lips. "Drink, baby. Let's celebrate. You successfully buried Maryanne, last night, didn't you?" Before he could respond in the negative, she went on: "Yes, I know you did, because you didn't call me to say anything went wrong. I was worried about you for a long time last night while I was working, because you didn't call me. I thought the cops had nabbed you."

She paused to drink some of the wine herself, which reassured Bob a little, but before he could correct her mistaken impression of the success of their 'dead wife burial' project, she resumed speaking: "I'm glad that's over with now. Now we can move on with our life together. Did you see the posts I put up on Facebook? 'Maryanne' is currently holidaying with imaginary friends in Venezuela."

"I'm worried about that," Bob managed to say, relieved that for the moment at least, Ashley seemed to have forgotten she wanted to whip him again. "And I still don't see why she couldn't just go to Acapulco like we'd initially planned to do. But even overlooking that, Maryanne can't remain in Venezuela forever. Sooner or later, someone will—"

"Stop worrying and have some more wine, baby," Ashley said, holding the glass to Bob's lips again. Then she leaned forward and kissed him deeply, sticking her tongue so far into his mouth that he almost choked on it. With the hand that wasn't holding the wineglass, she delicately stroked the back of his neck.

Bob felt his cock thump in his pants and wondered what was the matter with him. *This is neither the time, nor the place, nor the state of affairs. And to tell the truth, this isn't the right woman either.*

But his body seemed not to care. As Ashley continued kissing him, his penis seemed to be willing him to strip her clothes off and do her on the couch; an impulse he violently resisted.

Ashley finally pulled her tongue out of his mouth. "Where was I? Yeah, don't sweat it about Maryanne vacationing in Venezuela. You're gonna love what I've got planned for her there."

"What *do* you have planned for her?"

But Ashley wagged a finger in his face, and made him drink some more wine. "Hey, I forgot to ask earlier: You did bury Maryanne well away from Brian Chu's grave, didn't you?"

Seeing as she was holding the wineglass to his lips, meaning he couldn't immediately speak, Ashley seemed to assume his silence between gulps was a reply in the affirmative. "Well, that's good then."

Bob now stared intently at Ashley's face. He wondered if she was high on narcotics; which would explain why she wasn't giving him any chance to speak.

And he was already feeling drowsy again. As Bob's mind fogged over, he realized that Ashley had tricked him.

Oh no, she only had one little sip of wine and I've drunk almost the entire glass!

He was fading fast now, but he looked at Ashley, and saw that she was smiling back at him.

"Let . . . let me go . . . monster . . . monster," he said weakly.

"No, I'm not a monster," Ashley replied airily, standing up from his thighs and parting her nightie so her body was nicely on display. "I'm just a young woman who can only get sexual gratification by hurting others."

"Monster . . . monster."

"Oh, shut up, darling, and don't be difficult. We have an agreement. I've more than kept my side of the bargain, and so you've got to keep yours. You know the saying: No pain equals no gain. You stand to benefit a great deal if you let me hurt you."

"Ugh . . . monst . . ." Bob's tongue gave up trying. He'd left things much too late.

Ashley's gaze narrowed. "Hey, call me a monster one more time, and tonight I'll go *really* hard on you."

Bob no longer had any control over his limbs or lips; all he could do was fight to keep his eyes open; a fight he was already losing.

"Don't worry, honey," Ashley said sweetly as his eyes closed. "I'm not going to whip you tonight. Tonight, we're going to be doing something completely different; something I've wanted to try out for ages, but that asshole Tony never let me. Oh, tonight is gonna be a whole lot more fun than yesterday was. For me, at least, if not for you."

Her tinkling laughter accompanied Bob to sleep.

CHAPTER 31

Bob woke up again in the same room as last night, but with one major difference: This time he was bound to the other X-Frame.

The first thing Bob noticed on waking up, was Ashley seated in a portable chair opposite him. The second thing he noticed was that he once again had a gag-ball in his mouth. Possibly the same one as yesterday, from the taste of it.

Tonight, Ashley was completely naked and also barefoot. She leaned back in her chair and it unfolded like a recliner, lowering her torso and head and raising her legs. Ashley's left hand gripped a silver vibrator; her right hand clutched a small device like a remote control.

"Hello, honey," Ashley said on seeing he was awake. She waved the vibrator at him. "Time to have our fun."

Bob's mind cleared quickly now and he realized that he was once again naked.

It now occurred to him that while the drug Ashley had spiked his wine with was fast-acting, its effects weren't long-lasting. There would be no benefit for her in knocking him out if he didn't wake up quickly afterwards so she could have her fun with him; or, if the anesthetic dulled the pain she wished him to feel. Bob could practically feel the narcotic wearing off now. Just like yesterday, the departure of the chemical from his system left him in a state of tense apprehension.

The realization that he was in some physical discomfort made him look down at himself. In horror, he saw what Ashley had done to him.

The crocodile clips that he'd yesterday noticed attached to this particular X-Frame were now all clamped on his body. Two of them were attached to his nipples, and others were attached to pinches of skin on his belly and thighs. A wired metal cock-ring throttled the root of his penis and also encircled his testicles. There were no clamps on either his hands or feet, but both of these omissions were easily explained: for whatever reason, he was standing inside of a wide metal tray, to the edges of which electric wires had been attached, and looking up, he saw that the metal bangles that secured his wrists were also wired.

He stared at Ashley in horror. Oh, God, no!

"I call this invention of mine 'Electric Sex,' " Ashley said and pressed a button on the remote control. "Let's enjoy it together."

In what was either a predetermined or a random sequence, the multitude of electrodes attached to Bob's body began shocking him. While Ashley manipulated the controls of the remote, Bob jerked in pain, first one way and then another, while his tormentor simultaneously parted the lips of her vagina and began pleasuring herself with the dildo.

Bob screamed and screamed in his mind. There was no respite. First one part of his body would feel the agony, and then another; and at times all of him would feel like he was being fried. His penis alternatively felt alive and dead. The soles of his feet would first feel like they were being boiled and then like they were frozen.

It was absolute total torment; torment that seemed to last for hours, while Ashley spent the entire time masturbating in front of him, fondling herself, squeezing her breasts, and pleasuring herself with the dildo till she came and came again.

Bob stared at her in the wonder of agony, hardly conscious of her existence in the room, or of the existence of the room itself, fully conscious of nothing but pain and more pain, of the endless jolts of electricity jerking through his system; none of them sufficient to kill him, but each one more than sufficient to recreate the sensation of being tased over and over again. He knew that he was losing his mind.

The shocking voltage wasn't constant either, but fluctuated up and down, regulated by whatever control Ashley had worked into her remote-control dimmer thingummyjig. Occasionally, when Bob seemed to be fading away into unconsciousness, or when Ashley just wanted to excite herself a bit more, she would temporarily let go of the silver dildo in her sex, and then, as if she was playing a video game, depress sequences of buttons on her remote control with both hands, which would cause additional jewels of electric pain to flow into Bob's body.

By the time it was over and Ashley released him, Bob had both shit and pissed himself more than once, and had also vomited through and around the gag-ball. The metal tray below him was full of his waste bodily fluids. He was a mess, but he didn't care. He just wanted to be gone from there.

Ashley apparently didn't care either, having had multiple orgasms during his hour or so of torment. Now that she was sexually satiated, she released Bob from the electrified X-Frame, helped him into the bathroom that adjoined her torture chamber, and left him under the shower, where he couldn't stand up but slumped down in the corner, trembling as if the electrocution was still going on.

"I hate you," he told her. "You are completely evil."

"Don't be silly, darling, no one ever hates their guardian angel," she replied with a smile. "You utterly love me. You just don't realize it yet."

He stared at her without understanding.

"Clean yourself off while I mop the floor," she added in a kind voice. "Then I'll order us both some pizza for dinner."

She passed him a sponge and watched him soap himself for a while, then left him alone.

CHAPTER 32

Bob awoke in his own bed the next morning. His muscles ached like crazy and for the first few minutes after getting up he tottered on his feet like his ears were damaged.

He groaned each time he remembered last night.

Yep, I've always known sadists were perverts, but Ashley takes the meaning of the word to new extremes. Shocking extremes. What's most bothering of all is how she keeps professing that she's in love with me, when all I can think of is escaping as far away from her as I can.

Electric shock left no physical scars. But Bob still felt numb, almost as numb as he had last night when staggering down the stairs to his front door. He and Ashley had shared a pizza and then, unable to stand being in the same room with her for much longer, he'd told her he needed to go, because he had some office work to handle on his laptop this morning.

She'd sighed wistfully when he'd departed.

The welts from his lashing itched. He'd forgotten to collect the anesthetic salve from Ashley.

He'd been so desperate to get away from her after she'd tortured him that he'd still not mentioned to her what was going on with Maryanne's corpse, as doing so would have delayed him there, possibly for hours, because at first Ashley certainly wouldn't have believed his story, and afterwards she would have insisted on coming down here to confirm things for herself; and then it might have proven impossible to separate from her. After being shocked that viciously with electricity, flight had seemed more important to Bob than explaining to his mad tormentor that they had a huge problem in his condo.

Thinking on it now, Bob decided to keep his mouth shut about Maryanne's reanimated corpse for the time being. Yes, she was a creepy sight, but so far, the demon fetus inside her wasn't hurting anyone, and he suspected it wouldn't make a nuisance of itself so long as he kept feeding it.

He also thought that it must be hungry by now. Time to feed the beast.

But first of all, he checked his cellphone notifications. The first thing he did was open up Facebook.

He had to smile. 'Maryanne' had posted three vacation updates from the Venezuelan capital Caracas, in the last of which she claimed she'd 'reveal something very interesting to everyone in the next day or two.' Bob was as curious as Maryanne's Facebook friends were as to what her big reveal would be. Once more she'd uploaded some videos of herself, complete with her voice, though slightly garbled. The sheer 'authenticity' of those videos shocked Bob.

"The original video images of Maryanne were all taken from her cellphone and laptop, and then I manipulated them with CGI and AI," Ashley had explained last night during their pizza dinner.

Bob also had several messages from colleagues at work, and one message from his mother, who lived nearby in Springfield. His mother wanted him to call her. Bob suspected this had something to do with the preparations for his younger sister Linda's upcoming wedding.

Bob winced, on remembering that Maryanne was supposed to be a bridesmaid at Linda's wedding.

This particular situation has to be handled with care or it might blow up in my face.

Bob felt relieved that Maryanne herself had only one surviving relative; the senile old uncle who'd raised her from childhood, and who now lived in a retirement home cum mental health facility in Fitchburg, in the north of the state.

Okay, now it's feeding time!

Through with social media for the time being, Bob went to his kitchen, got some raw meat out of the fridge, and went to the bathroom. He peeked in, noticed that Maryanne was still pacing aimlessly, and then slid the meat across the floor to her. When she turned toward it, he saw that her pregnancy bulge was much bigger this morning.

Once again, he shut the door before she squatted over the meat. No point seeing *that* each time he fed the thing inside her.

Now that he was satisfied that the demon fetus inside his dead wife was satisfied, Bob returned to the kitchen and made himself breakfast.

Likely as a result of Ashley's last torture session, Bob discovered he was very hungry. He heaped a plate full with scrambled eggs, loaded a tray with bread and jam, and carried the whole thing out to the living room, along with a steaming mug of coffee.

Trying to create a semblance of normalcy amidst chaos, while eating he turned on the TV and watched it for a bit. He didn't know which was in more confusion, the world or his own life.

A gentle cellphone beep announced a fresh Facebook notification. Bob looked at it. It was another update from Maryanne; a grinning picture of her having breakfast in a restaurant and the statement: "Yeah . . . having the time of my life here in sunny Caracas. Hey, honey, get here already! I'm missing you."

Bob spent a long time staring at this picture. It disturbed him, because he now got the feeling that creating and manipulating the existence of this fictional Maryanne person consisted of more than simply Ashley rendering assistance to him.

No, she seems to enjoy this. She's not just a physical sadist but a psychological one too. I think Ashley enjoys messing with people's minds as much as she enjoys hurting their bodies.

In Facebook-land people were already 'liking' Maryanne's new post and commenting on it. To create the right impression, Bob quickly posted a comment: "Still too tired to fly, honey, but I'll be down there with ya in a couple days. Love and miss you too! Xoxo."

Yeah, that looks about right, he thought, suddenly understanding that his entire life might just have slipped out of his control.

CHAPTER 33

Today was Saturday. Bob would have liked to head out to town like he'd done yesterday, but he ached too badly to drive. His muscles felt little better than jelly. He decided to spend the rest of the day watching TV.

Yes, he did realize that watching television was a dumb thing to do when you had a dead body to get rid of, but, considering how far things had skewed out of left field, what else could he do?

Out of more sensible alternatives, he lounged on the couch and looked for a pro wrestling program.

He'd just found one when the doorbell rang. Bob muted the television and went to see who was ringing. He dreaded it being Ashley.

But instead, it was Ashley's mother Jennifer at the door. Bob had more or less been expecting her to visit. He invited her in.

"Can I get you some coffee?" he asked.

When she replied in the affirmative, he went into the kitchen for a few moments to brew it.

***

While making the coffee, Bob considered telling Jennifer about his problem. He knew that Jennifer considered herself a witch, and so maybe she could help him.

Things like my current problem—having a pregnant blue undead wife in my bathroom should be right up her alley. I'm sure witches deal with similar situations all the time.

But then, he cautioned himself.

But what if I'm wrong? What if her entire witchcraft thing is merely a pose? What if, on seeing Maryanne, Jennifer goes into total freak-out mode and calls the police on me? Or worse still, what if she at first pretends to help me out, and then once she's safely away from me, she then goes and phones the police? And, considering that Jennifer and Maryanne were good friends, that's very likely to happen. No, it's best that I just leave Jennifer out of this. I've already involved her daughter in Maryanne's death—no point making my crime a Haskins family affair.

Sighing that there seemed to be no rest for the misunderstood as well as the wicked, Bob finished brewing the coffee and headed back to the living room.

***

"Thanks," Jennifer said when he handed her the steaming mug. "I just came by to see how you're doing."

"I'm okay, I guess," Bob replied, though he suddenly felt very uneasy. Jennifer was looking at him oddly, as if trying to determine his state of mental health. Or, did she perhaps suspect that something was wrong?

"So, have you called Maryanne yet?" Bob asked her.

Jennifer shook her head. "I tried to yesterday afternoon, but couldn't get through." She was still staring oddly at Bob. "There was a little something she was supposed to see me about before she left. Nothing serious though—I'll just handle it by myself. That was part of the reason I really wanted to get her on the phone."

Bob pointed the remote control at the TV and turned it off. "Yeah, you know what communications are supposedly like in third-world countries. I called her both yesterday and this morning, but I mostly got static and could hardly make out what she was saying."

Jennifer frowned. "But I thought you both were going to Acapulco for your vacation. That's what Maryanne kept telling me."

"You're not going to believe this, but Maryanne changed our destination behind my back. I don't completely blame her; you know how overworked I've been of late. By the time I found out about it, Maryanne had rebooked everything. Our flights, hotels, itinerary; everything."

Jennifer lowered her mug of coffee. "I wonder why she'd go and do a thing like that?"

"She said she no longer felt safe going to Acapulco," Bob lied. "She said she'd read too many online news stories of American tourists being kidnapped or killed by the drug cartels down there."

Jennifer didn't seem convinced by this. "I dunno, Bob. Something about her behavior strikes me as fishy. I mean, consider the way she just took off yesterday without you, and without even saying goodbye to me either."

Bob had no need to fake a troubled expression now; he really was bothered that Jennifer suspected foul play. If Jennifer enquired about how they'd gotten new visas, he'd been sunk.

I haven't spoken to Jennifer in a while either, so how did she know I'm home alone now? No, that much was evident from Maryanne's posts. Or, Ashley might even have mentioned that to her.

"To tell you the truth, Jennifer, I'm really concerned myself," Bob said. "As far as I can tell, Venezuela is just as violent as Mexico; if not more so."

"Well, you'll be joining her in a few days," Jennifer said. "She'll be much safer with both of you there."

Jennifer resumed drinking her coffee and Bob relaxed. He realized that his worries were unfounded and that Jennifer was simply concerned for her friend's safety in a foreign country.

Jennifer finished her coffee and got up. "I gotta be going now. Got a few things to do around the house. Chris was taking a nap, so I decided to pop downstairs and see you. I hope he's not woken up yet."

"How's Chris doing?" Bob asked as he saw Jennifer to the door. "I saw you guys going out yesterday. To the doctor's, was it?"

Jennifer shook her head sadly. "He's still the same, Bob. I really wish he'd get better. Then we can all have some fun times again like we used to do."

Still shaking her head, she walked off to the elevator.

Bob felt really sad for her. Jennifer was a nice woman. And her husband Chris had been a good friend of his too.

CHAPTER 34

Before Bob could once more get comfortable with the television, the doorbell rang again.

This time the caller was Rodney, who lived downstair.

"Hey, come on in, bro," Bob told him and turned back into the house, leaving Rodney to shut the door behind him.

Rodney Sherrick was a tall and fat guy in his mid-twenties. Over the past year, he and Bob had become firm friends. Rodney partly owned a video store along with a cousin of his, and spent most of his spare time doing video reviews of new movies on the internet.

Rodney lumbered his way into Bob's living room, planted his large frame on the couch, and leaned back like he owned the place.

"Got any cold beer?" he asked.

"I'll go have a look," Bob said and left for the kitchen.

He searched through the fridge, found several cans of Bud Light at the rear of the lowest shelf, and returned to the living room with two of them.

In his absence Rodney had turned the TV back on and was watching an old WCW match, Bret 'The Hitman' Hart versus 'Nature Boy' Rick Flair, with the sound off.

Bob had a moment's worry that since they were drinking beers, Rodney might soon need to take a piss, and he couldn't have him using the guest bathroom.

No problem. I'll tell Rod the flusher's broken and to use the one in our bedroom instead.

"Hey, catch," Bob said and lobbed a can of Bud Light at Rodney.

"Thanks, bro," Rodney said, snatching the beer out of the air like he was Stone Cold Steve Austin. He pulled the tab, took a good long swig, and then licked his lips. "Yeah, that definitely hit the spot."

Then he looked away from the television and focused his attention on Bob. "So, what's been going on with ya? I just got through reading Maryanne's latest Facebook posts. You guy's goin' through a rough patch, or what?"

"Forget it, bro," Bob retorted after swallowing. "You know how women act, don't you?"

Rodney laughed. "I can't honestly say I do."

Bob scowled at him. "Hey, be serious. One year on and I still can't tell if you're gay, asexual, too shy to ask a lady out on a date; . . . or if you just have a tiny dick and are scared of chicks finding out about it."

"Screw you, bro. My dick's fine. No micropenis shit happening here."

"So why haven't I ever seen you with a girlfriend then? There's loads of hot women that come to that video store of yours. And I'm sure you meet many more at those endless horror conventions you attend. How come you never get together with any of 'em?"

Rodney rolled his eyes at the ceiling. "One of these days I'm gonna surprise you." Then he frowned. "But . . . we were discussing *your* fantastic sex life, not my lack of one."

"Yeah, that's true," Bob agreed. Both men stared at the silent TV for a while.

In classic wrestling heel fashion, the Nature Boy had just poked the Hitman in the eyes, and then, when the referee's back was turned, hit the Hitman with a low blow where it would hurt him the most. Then, the Nature Boy called the distracted ref's attention to the fact that the Hitman was down on the mat, and tried to pin him. The Hitman recovered quickly, however, and rolled the Nature Boy up in a small package finisher. The referee counted one . . . two . . . three, and the match was over. The Hitman had stripped the Nature Boy of his latest championship belt.

The show cut to a commercial break and Bob and Rodney looked at one another again.

"So . . ." Rodney prompted.

"It's like I was saying. You know how women behave. Maryanne's miffed at me 'cos I said I was too tired to travel when she wanted to."

Rodney pointed his beer can at Bob. "Why didn't she just wait till you felt better? Hell, you're the one who needs a vacation, not her. All she does is laze around the place."

"Hey, hey," Bob grumbled. "Go easy on her. I'm the only one allowed to complain about Maryanne. If you need a woman to bitch about, marry a wife of your own."

Rodney waved his hands at Bob. "Yeah, yeah, I know she's getting ready for maternity and all that—whatever that means."

"You don't know 'cos you don't have a wife. Go get your in-the-closet ass married."

Rodney faked a pained expression. "Ouch, bro, that hurts like a dick in the ass. Hey, hey, listen. What I'm trying to say is—Maryanne has effectively been on vacation since she quit working. So . . . why the hell was she in such a rush to leave for Venezuela before you did? And why Venezuela? Wasn't it supposed to be Mexico?"

Bob faked nonchalance. "I don't know, and I don't freakin' care. Don't you get started on any conspiracy theories about Maryanne. I'm more concerned about her safety down there."

Rodney waved a dismissive hand at Bob. "Nothing to worry about. Us Americans are always giving foreign countries a bad rep about kidnappings and stuff. It's 'cos of films like *Taken*, and such like. *Black Hawk Down* and all those military propaganda flicks. Hollywood is programming us to be paranoid. It's so we'll go along like sheep when POTUS Biden wants to bomb someone."

"Spare me both the indy filmmaker B.S. and your MAGA rhetoric," Bob retorted, then got to his feet. "Hey, you want another beer?"

Rodney laughed a deep belly laugh and nodded. Bob headed for the kitchen to fetch two more cans of Bud Light. Shooting the shit with Rodney was doing him a hell of a lot of good. It was exactly what he needed to help him temporarily forget the blue abomination that lurked in his bathroom.

He returned with the beers and a pack of potato chips. The vintage wrestling show was still on. The guys turned up the volume and watched Sting and Goldberg competing for the WCW world title. It was a hell of a fight.

CHAPTER 35

Today seemed a day for visitors. No sooner had Rodney left for the video store, saying he'd call on Bob tonight so they could watch the basketball game, than the doorbell rang again.

Bob warily peeped through the spyhole. It wasn't Ashley this time either. This time it was Amanda, the lady who lived in the other condo on this floor.

"Hey there," Amanda said once he'd opened the door. "Is it okay if I come in for a minute?"

Bob nodded. "Please do."

Following behind Amanda as she walked into the living room, Bob wondered why she would be coming to visit him. She was really Maryanne's friend. And she had to know that Maryanne was currently out of the country. But then, Amanda was a nosy woman. She was always fishing around for details of other people's lives. She wasn't here simply to enquire about his health as had been the case with both Jennifer and Rodney's visits.

Amanda Fenton was a small and pretty woman, with long brown hair and sparkling blue eyes. Bob could clearly see what her boyfriend Marvin saw in her; the mystery was what she saw in the thuggish Marvin. He put it down to the age-old adage that 'opposites attract.'

Once Amanda was seated, Bob was about offering her a cup of coffee. But Amanda preempted this by speaking first:

"I don't like intruding like this, Bob," she said pressing her fingers together on her belly. "But I can't get Maryanne either on Facebook or on the phone, for a WhatsApp call. I'm wondering if you know what's wrong."

"The phone setup's a mess down there," Bob quickly agreed. "But she should be able to reply you on WhatsApp and Facebook." After saying this, he made a mental note to point this out to Ashley.

She needs to answer a few of the PMs Maryanne will be receiving, like those from my sister Linda and my mom—all she has to do is forward the incoming message to me and I'll compose an appropriate response for her. And the same goes

96

for WhatsApp messages too. What I'll do is make her a list of Maryanne's close friends, so she'll know which messages are the important ones.

"Well, that's okay then," Amanda said.

"Can I make you a cup of coffee?" Bob asked.

But Amanda didn't reply. Bob realized that Amanda was studying his face carefully, scrutinizing him like he was a book. This was the second time today that this had happened. Jennifer too had spent quite a while studying his face. It was starting to make him feel uncomfortable again.

"Why are you staring at me like that?" he finally asked.

"You don't seem bothered," Amanda said. "I can't understand it. You and Maryanne seemed so happy together. And she never mentioned to me that the two of you were having any marital problems."

"What are you talking about?" Bob asked. "I really don't know what you're talking about."

Now Amanda looked worried. "Oh, my God. You don't know then?"

"Know what?" Bob had no need to act confused. He *was* confused.

Amanda pointed to his cellphone. "When last did you check your Facebook updates?"

"About two hours ago? Why?"

"Check them now." She nodded at him. "Go on. Check Maryanne's Facebook timeline now."

Bob did so. Maryanne had two new Facebook posts. The first of these was simply another shot of her, wearing a straw hat and looking radiant, with a gorgeous tropical landscape in the background.

But the second update was the one that made Bob gape. This update showed Maryanne with a muscular man, whose face she'd X-ed out.

"Okay, friends, here's that major reveal I was talking about. I can't go on living a lie. My heart has been elsewhere for a year now, and I can't live like this anymore. I'm letting everyone know now that I'm leaving my husband Bob for the real love of my life, MARIO!!!! Wish us the best, everyone."

Bob looked at Amanda. "What the hell is this about?"

Amanda seemed surprised by the question. "Bob, don't ask me. She's *your* wife."

"Yeah, she is . . . she was . . . she . . . I don't get what's happening, that's all."

Bob found it strange how well he was playing the part of the cuckolded husband. But then, he wasn't really playing a part. He was completely shocked by the direction Ashley had swung her drama in, and his natural confusion made it easy for him to pretend to be confused.

"How could she do this to me?" he asked Amanda. "We were so happy. She wanted to have a baby, that's all."

Amanda, assuming that Bob really needed comforting, moved over to his side and took his hand. Bob noted that she seemed genuinely sympathetic, not like someone who was delighted she had a new sob-story to gossip about.

"I'm sorry, Bob, but things like this do happen to us."

"But, Amanda, we were so happy."

Amanda laughed. "I thought I was happy too, right up to the moment my sonofabitch husband served me with divorce papers."

Yes, Bob remembered that. Amanda had been previously been married to a wealthy lawyer, but then her husband divorced her and bought her this condo as part of the divorce settlement. If Bob remembered correctly, Amanda now got a monthly sum of money that would continue for the next ten years at least. Unless she remarried before then, when the whole remaining amount would be paid to her as a lump sum.

That may be great motivation for her to marry Marvin. Or maybe not to marry him.

"But . . . but . . ." he gasped as if his heart was breaking.

Amanda gently placed a hand on his shoulder. "Take it easy, take it easy. Listen, can I get you anything? Some water perhaps?"

Bob shook his head, and quickly got to his feet. Remembering to keep a sad face, he said: "No, let me. I was just going to offer you coffee anyway."

"I'll go and make it," Amanda said. "You shouldn't be—"

"Trust me, let me do it," Bob countered. "You won't know where to look for everything." He scowled at his phone. "I still can't believe she's left me."

Amanda stared at him as if she was worried that he wanted to get a knife in the kitchen to commit suicide with.

To reassure her, Bob sighed deeply, and forced a smile. "I must really be a fool. I . . . I never saw it coming. But . . . Amanda . . . she's been dating this musclebound Mario jerk for a year now. How the hell did they meet?"

"Take it easy, man. Take it easy. Go make our coffee, and when you come back, we'll talk." Amanda frowned. "I still think you should let me do it, but since you insist and it is your house . . . Just don't hurt yourself in the kitchen."

"Damn you, Maryanne," Bob growled in fake fury and headed for the kitchen.

The real reason Bob was going to the kitchen was so he could think up a natural sounding sequence of lies to feed to Amanda.

Despite her sympathetic behavior, Bob knew that Amanda was actually pleased that now she wasn't the only divorced person living in their condominium, and was really here to learn as much about Maryanne's betrayal as possible.

Bob set the coffee to brew and dredged up plausible sounding scenarios from movies he'd watched:

Well, she had been spending an inordinate amount of time researching on Venezuela and Venezuelan arts and culture, but I never thought . . . She'd suggested naming our first child Mario or Maria, but I never suspected . . . Hmmm, now that I think about it, she had been acting coldly towards me. . . You know, once she told me I was no 'Latin lover' . . . and I also remember . . . damn, how in the hell could I have been so blind for so long? . . . And now just look what it's led up to.

CHAPTER 36

To Amanda's credit, she did feel genuinely sorry for Bob. She'd been through the same horrible experience, and you didn't come away from something like that without gaining a good deal of empathy for others in similar situations.

She'd read somewhere that the most traumatic, stressful thing that could happen in an individual's life was the death of a spouse, and then next was to get divorced. Amanda now knew this to be true.

Oh, I loved Dave Fenton with all my heart. I did everything for that man, and look where it got me! Discarded like a strip of tissue paper he'd wiped his ass with when that leggy stripper shook her ass in his face.

Now the 'leggy stripper' had the big house and the chauffeur-driven limo and two kids to boot, and Amanda was here, living on a mere pittance. Amanda should have gotten more from the divorce settlement, but she'd made the mistake of hiring one of ex-husband's protégés to represent her interests.

And, wow, did he help Dave screw me over. Never marry a lawyer; that's the first piece of advice I give my girlfriends now. Doctors are fine, at least you'll have a long and a healthy life; marry a dentist and you'll have the best teeth in town. Marry a grocery store owner and you'll be fat and buxom; a tailor and you're certain to be fashionable. Marry a plastic surgeon and you're assured of a knockout body for life. But lawyers? What exactly are they any good for? Pah, they're the shit of the earth!

She stopped her bitter reminiscence to think about Bob. He'd looked heartsick once she'd showed him the evidence of Maryanne's betrayal, and she felt very bad for having been the one to reveal to him just how fickle the human heart could be. She'd come here because she thought he'd already read Maryanne's nasty post.

Amanda wanted to question Maryanne about what was going on in her life. She desired to find out what had brought her to this crisis point and advise her not to throw a good love away in exchange for a bad one. What was the saying again? Better the devil you know than the angel you don't.

Too late for that now, I guess.

"Hey, Bob, are you okay in there?" she called out.

She got no reply and felt a little worried. She shouldn't have let him visit the kitchen alone. She'd been in there a few times, and knew that Maryanne had all sorts of knives in there.

"Yeah, I'm okay!" Bob finally replied. "Our coffee is almost ready."

Amanda felt relieved. But Bob had sounded miserable.

"Well, that's how life is sometimes," she told herself aloud. "After a while the pain will die away and he'll accept that one just has to roll with the punches."

Amanda wondered how exactly she would comfort Bob.

Maybe it'll be best to let Marvin do it. I should invite Bob over for dinner tonight like I suggested to Marvin, and let Marvin give him a man-to-man pep talk.

But she knew that wouldn't work out. Marvin was a man's man, a hard-as-nails biker who had no time for weakness in others. Marvin prided himself on being strong, and looked down on anyone who wasn't. As it was, Marvin called Bob a wimp behind his back, so there was no chance that he'd have any interest in comforting him.

Amanda had already called up Marvin at the bar where he worked and told him about Maryanne's betrayal. And what had been Marvin's response?

"Don't sweat it, baby. It had to happen sooner or later. A good-lookin' chick like that's got no business being with a loser like that." He'd laughed. "If it weren't that I already had you, honey, I'd have taken Maryanne away from Bob myself. A real woman needs a real man, that's what I say."

And that is the full extent of my darling macho man Marvin's empathy with his suffering fellow man, Amanda thought with a cold smile. *But still, he's better than Dave. A whole lot better than Dave.*

Then Amanda felt a twinge in her bladder.

Dammit, I need to pee.

Bob still hadn't emerged from the kitchen with their coffees, so Amanda got to her feet.

"Hey, Bob, I'm going to use your bathroom!"

She waited for his response, but none came, and so she decided to just head for the bathroom anyway. One peculiarity of this building having been converted from office space was that the condos all had different layouts. But Amanda knew where the bathroom was; she'd used it often when visiting Maryanne; it was right down the hallway.

It wasn't like she was intruding either; there was no one else at home, just Bob.

In any case, Amanda felt too pressed to wait. She felt like she was about to burst open.

Immediately Amanda stepped into the connecting hallway, she smelt it; a rotten odor as if a rat had died in a cupboard somewhere. The nasty odor was faint, but unmistakable.

Worryingly, the closer she got to the bathroom, the more the smell intensified, until Amanda suspected it was coming from inside there, and maybe she'd be better off dashing back home to use her own bathroom in her own condo, and returning afterwards to continue her talk with Bob.

Oh no, I'm too pressed; I'll just have to endure whatever mess I find in here. But how the hell is it that Bob can't smell this?

But, despite her dogged resolution to simply get her urinary business over with as quickly as possible, Amanda found herself pausing outside the bathroom door.

Oh my God, it smells as if a whole nest of rats died in there.

The bathroom door was locked, which was in itself odd. Amanda unlocked it, stepped inside the bathroom, and thought she had gone mad.

That's Maryanne. No, it isn't. Yes, it is. Why is her head hanging like that, and why is her skin all blue, and why does she look pregnant? And why, why, above all other things why, is Maryanne here at home, when everyone knows she's actually down in Venezuela with her hot new boyfriend Mario? And and and . . . . Amanda suddenly felt as if her brain was being squeezed. *What the hell is that thing coming out of her pussy?*

One mystery was however now resolved: The horrible rotting smell that had alerted Amanda that something was wrong in the bathroom was coming from chunks of maggot-infested meat scattered across the pink floor tiles, with some of the chunks looking as if they'd been partially digested and then vomited back out. Two bloody trails on Maryanne's blue thighs seemed to indicate where the meat had been regurgitated from.

Amanda still did not believe that those were blue *hands* dangling between her friend's legs.

"Maryanne, what the hell happened to you?" Amanda asked in a scared whisper. "Maryanne, speak to me."

But Maryanne just stared back at her with two dead eyes that were each the color of egg yolk, with both her blank facial expression and the blue skin of her face projecting an implacable evil.

Amanda, who was standing two steps into the bathroom, now backed away towards the bathroom door.

But then the strange blue-skinned Maryanne with the broken neck and bulging belly and the horrible protuberant yellow eyes stepped forward and grabbed Amanda tightly by her shoulders. What made this even more crazy was that Maryanne had somehow reached up and grabbed Amanda using the arms and hands coming from between her legs.

Amanda began screaming.

CHAPTER 37

The sound of Amanda's screaming broke Bob out of his mental reverie.

What the hell was that noise? Oh no, that's Amanda!

Bob ran out of the kitchen, through the living room, and down the hallway to the bathroom. The door to the guest bathroom was wide open, giving him a better-than-ringside view of the horror that was happening in there.

Dead Maryanne had a firm hold of Amanda's neck, only she was gripping Amanda's neck with her 'lower' set of hands, which of course didn't bode well for Amanda's wellbeing.

Maryanne was standing in the bathtub while Amanda was outside of it, down on the floor, gasping for breath. Amanda's neck was held tight against the edge of the bath, and her head was pressed tight against the dead woman's crotch.

Amanda had originally been trying to loosen Maryanne's grip on her neck. Immediately she spotted Bob, she stretched out her arms towards him instead.

"Help me!" she croaked helplessly, waving her hands at him. "She . . . she's . . . killing me!"

Bob could see that. As far as he could tell, Maryanne was trying to feed Amanda to the baby in her womb, except that Amanda's head was too big to fit into her sex. As if she was totally oblivious to his presence, Bob's blue-skinned dead wife had her hands braced behind her on the bathroom tiles, her spread blue knees braced on the edge of the bathtub, and was pulling hard on her frightened captive's neck, seemingly hard enough to break Amanda's neck if Bob did not quickly intervene.

So, Bob did intervene. First of all, he grabbed hold of Amanda's shoulders and tried to pull her away from Maryanne. But doing this only succeeded in tightening the grip on Amanda's neck, to the extent that now the fingers of Maryanne's 'lower' set of hands began digging into Amanda's flesh and drawing blood.

"Oh shit!" Amanda gasped in pain, as the ends of the blue fingers penetrated deeper into her body and blood seeped out around their nails. "Get her off of me!"

The blue fingers were wet and slimy, and Bob really didn't want to touch them. But now, realizing that he had no choice if he wanted to save Amanda's life, he let go of her shoulders and grabbed the hands instead.

However, once he made contact with Maryanne's body, he immediately felt the same repelling force that he had when he'd touched Maryanne after she had turned blue. The force threw him across the bathroom and left him sitting on the toilet seat.

Stunned, Bob could only watch what happened next.

The effort of dealing with Bob had distracted Maryanne, and so caused her to lessen the tightness of her hold on Amanda's throat. Amanda seized this opportunity with a wild attempt at breaking free. But Maryanne reacted quickly and tightened her grip again, which was Amanda's undoing, as, before she was halfway to her feet, she was yanked violently back down against the edge of the bathtub.

Bob heard a loud 'snap' reminiscent of Maryanne's own death, and then Amanda Fenton, her neck broken too, collapsed dead beside the bathtub.

Bob stared in disbelief. This was the worst possible thing that could have happened.

No, no, no, no, no!

Now that Amanda was dead, the strange drama continued. The blue hands resumed tying to feed her head into Maryanne's vagina.

Bob watched this for a short interval. At first, he felt very scared and very sorry for what had happened to Amanda, who after all, was a friend. But as he watched 'Maryanne' pull Amanda's corpse fully into the bathtub and continue trying to 'eat' it between her legs, he began to grow angry. This waste of life, this obscenity he was witnessing— his having to deal with Ashley's sadist behavior—everything overloaded in his mind.

Bob staggered to his feet and walked down to his bedroom to fetch his gun.

He got the gun, cocked back the slide, made certain the safety catch was off, and then headed back to the guest bathroom. His plan was simple: to kill whatever was living and growing inside Maryanne's body.

That damn thing animating her is the reason for Amanda's death. Amanda didn't do anything to deserve being killed like that; all she likely wanted to do was use the bathroom. Amanda was simply a friend who came to check on my wellbeing.

The way Bob viewed it, he now had two deaths on his conscience. The knowledge that neither death was intentional hardly made him feel better.

I'll shoot it inside Maryanne's body, and then I'll call the police, and let them decide what to make of things!

Gun in hand he walked slowly now. Silent as a cat. He didn't want to startle the demonic baby growing inside Maryanne. Bob had no idea if the evil thing knew what a gun was, but if it did, this time it might resort to more than just throwing him across the room to protect itself.

Oh, my God—I'm such a fool, Bob thought suddenly. *Ever since Maryanne turned blue like this, she's been living evidence. I should have just called the police and let the authorities handle things. They'd have been as confused as I am.*

Well, it wasn't too late to make amends.

Hell, he thought, looking at the gun in his hands, *I don't even need to shoot it. I can just call the police now! All I need to do is lock Maryanne in the bathroom. When the police find her, they'll know she killed Amanda, and that I didn't!*

But three things stopped Bob from simply locking the door on Maryanne and Amanda and dialing 9-1-1.

Firstly, he couldn't even begin to count the number of supernatural-themed movies he'd watched in which the ghost or specter or demon only revealed itself to the person it desired to torment. Bob was certain that if he called the police, by the time they got here, Maryanne's corpse would once more be lying dead in the bathtub and rotting away like all well-behaved corpses do, and it wouldn't be blue in color or pregnant either, with a set of hands poking out from between its legs.

I'll be back to square one; though I might now be locked up as insane instead of being sent to the penitentiary.

Secondly, he also had Ashley to consider. He'd dragged her into this and made her an accessory to Maryanne's very suspicious-looking demise, and calling the police now would very likely get her into big trouble with them.

Maybe her CIA contacts will keep her out of doing time for helping me, but maybe they'll simply throw her under the bus, particularly if she ever whipped any of them as sadistically as she whipped me! And I'm very certain the crazy woman has. Who knows, maybe her ex Tony was even CIA.

So, maybe this was being unfair to Amanda, but Bob thought that involving the police in things at this juncture would be even more unfair to Ashley, who (her own fault though) had no idea that Maryanne's body was still down here.

So those were the first two reasons why Bob didn't simply once more lock Maryanne in the bathroom and dial 9-1-1.

The third reason?

When Bob reached the bathroom again, another change had taken place. The already surreal situation in there had just gotten more absurd.

Maryanne and Amanda were both still in the bathtub. Only now, Maryanne was no longer trying to eat Amanda. Instead, Amanda was now stretched out beneath Maryanne, who lay on top of her with her blue legs parted wide and her spread feet up on either rim of the bathtub, and with her blue hands similarly gripping opposite bathtub edges, and with her expressionless blue face pressed hard against the interior of the bath.

Maryanne's belly was contracting and expanding.

Bob quickly understood what this meant. *It's coming! The baby is coming out!*

This was so unexpected that Bob's mind drew a total blank as to his next course of action. Yes, one naturally expected pregnant women to give birth. But not *dead* pregnant women.

I should have known something like this would happen. Her belly has steadily been growing in size since I've been feeding it meat. What did I think would be the end result of that?

Maryanne's sex was already expanding, and the 'baby' was emerging. If it could reasonably be called a 'baby.'

The thing that emerged from Maryanne's womb was completely blue in color and slimy. It had a large head, those two long arms that Bob was already so familiar with from its feeding times, and a short stumpy body that ended in two deformed feet with almost no legs in-between. The creature lacked any visible sexual organs and as such seemed to be neither male nor female. It had batwing-like ears on its giant head, two huge yellow eyes with snake-eye pupils, and it lacked a nose. As Bob gaped at it, the thing opened its mouth and grinned at him. Without exaggeration, its mouth reached from ear to ear and was filled with hideous interlocking teeth. Its blue tongue was as warty as a toad's back.

Tellingly, the ugly thing wasn't attached to its mother by an umbilical cord.

Because Amanda was underneath Maryanne, the little monster lay there on her knees, then it rolled over and stood up.

It's a demon baby, Bob slowly realized as it righted itself to a full height of about two feet tall. *Maryanne has given birth to a demon baby.*

While he continued gaping at the demon baby, so perplexed by its horrifying appearance that he didn't even remember the gun in his hand, the creature turned around and sank its teeth into Maryanne's left leg. It bit down and Maryanne's left shin and foot clattered down into the bathtub, because the demon baby had bitten all the way through her leg. Only half of Maryanne's thigh remained connected to her body, ending in a truncated circle of seeping red meat around a smaller white circle of bone.

The demon baby noisily chewed and swallowed the portion of leg in its mouth, then it picked up the severed foot from between Amanda's knees and ate that too.

FOOD! FOOD! its deep mental voice chimed in delight in Bob's head.

Then it turned its attention to consuming the rest of Maryanne.

"Get away from her!" Bob shrieked when he saw what was happening. "Don't you dare eat her!"

He leapt on the disgusting blue infant and slammed the grip of his gun on its head, then tried to drag it away from Maryanne's body. But, with its teeth buried deep in Maryanne's belly, the baby backhanded Bob. He went flying again, this time landing outside in the hallway.

This is proving to be literally the most fucked-up day of my life, Bob thought while groaning in pain, as through the bathroom door he watched the demon baby eat Maryanne, its teeth biting through her bones as easily as they severed her flesh. The baby's mouth stretched wide like a snake's to consume her flesh; and either its jaws dislocated just as easily as those of the aforementioned serpent or weren't connected to each other at all, because it swallowed giant chunks of Maryanne in one go.

The hell with this—it can't eat my wife! I'll just shoot it!

Bob felt around for his gun, but it was nowhere to be found. Determined to put an end once and for all to this atrocity he was witnessing, he pulled himself up from the hallway floor, and gripping the wall for support, pulled himself back towards the bathroom. His only thought was to stop the demon baby eating Maryanne. The act seemed blasphemous to him, as if, being a creature from hell, eating her was in turn consigning her to a hell in its belly.

So, Bob staggered towards the bathroom, looking for his gun. He reached the bathroom door and, gripping its frame, peeked inside, keeping well out of range of the demon baby's arms. The baby meanwhile ignored him—it showed not the least concern that he was watching it. It was giving its mother's body its complete attention, and, Bob disgustedly observed, had so far eaten all of her up to her chest.

Because one woman's corpse lay beneath the other, this was a surreal sight, a magic trick in which the naked Maryanne was vanishing to reveal the clothed Amanda.

Bob scanned the bathroom floor for his gun, but saw no sign of it.

Which meant the weapon had dropped into the bathtub and now lay beneath the demon baby, which was the one place Bob was not about to search. And because the baby was standing on top of Amanda, that meant the gun was most likely wedged somewhere underneath Amanda's corpse.

Bob could already see that there was no point to his continuing his search for the firearm anyway. Having finished its slow and methodical consumption of both of her arms, the demon baby had just picked up Maryanne's head. It spread its mouth wide, so wide that its squat body looked like a funnel, dropped Maryanne's head into that funnel, and chewed and swallowed.

And that was the last that Bob saw of his late wife.

Then the demon baby sat down on Amanda's head and burped. Neither its body nor belly were any larger than they had been when it had birthed itself. When it looked towards Bob, he ducked away behind the bathroom door. He was still taken aback by how 'efficiently' the little blue monster had disposed of its mother.

The monster looked away and Bob peeked back into the bathroom. Once more he attempted to locate his gun. He concluded that it had to be wedged between Amanda's body and the interior of the bathtub, on the farther side of the demon infant. Amanda, meanwhile was soaked in Maryanne's blood.

Fuck if I'm gonna search under there, Bob thought.

The blue demon baby now began eating Amanda. This too was so unexpected that Bob had to watch it. The baby consumed Amanda with the same gross savagery that it had applied to Maryanne, starting at her head and proceeding slowly downward. It ate her clothes along with her. The baby went slower this time, however, as if its infernal hunger was partially appeased. But still, it seemed to have no intention of letting any part of Amanda Fenton go to waste.

Wow! Bob thought suddenly.

He'd just realized that the demon baby was getting rid of all the evidence for him. Yes, Maryanne's body—which he'd so far been unable to get rid of—was now gone for good, vanished into whatever bottomless pit the demon baby had for a stomach. And soon Amanda would be just as gone for good too.

And because, where there's no baby . . . I mean, no body . . . there's no crime, I'll be off the hook, completely free. Except . . . where's Amanda's cellphone? Did she have it on her when she came in here to pee? That can still be traced to me.

After peeking inside the bathtub and seeing no sign of Amanda's phone, Bob hurried back to the living room to look for it. He found the cellphone lying on the couch where Amanda had been sitting. He picked it up and rushed back to the bathroom. He realized that in this case speed was imperative. Even though the demon baby had been eating slower this time, it was already swallowing Amanda's right arm when Bob had left the bathroom. He needed to stick the cellphone somewhere on Amanda before the creature ate up all of her pockets.

The baby was eating Amanda's innards when Bob returned, scooping them out of her abdomen by the red handful and dropping them into its mouth. By now the bathtub was flooded with Amanda's blood, which was being prevented from draining away because her right heel was plugging the drain.

The blue baby turned and regarded Bob. He winced at the sharpness of its interlocking teeth, and at the intestines dangling from them, with the tips of several of its teeth poking through the pale gut flesh. He was horrified by the alienness of the baby's gaze and the seemingly endless appetite that its mind projected at him.

But Bob had a job to do here. He had to stick Amanda's cellphone into one of the pockets of her jeans before the demon got to them. He really didn't want to approach that close to the monster, but he had no choice but to do so.

Once the demon turned away again and scooped out another handful of Amanda's guts, Bob went into action. He stepped up close to the bathtub and carefully reached under the baby, doing his best not to touch its slimly little body and being ready to leap back to safety the moment it made any attempt to grab him.

Unable to conveniently maneuver the phone into Amanda's nearer pocket, he contented himself with slipping it into her waistband instead. Doing so, however, meant he had to reach further beneath the baby, and as he pulled his hand back, his wrist brushed against the baby's blue skin.

Its skin felt normal enough, but touching it filled Bob with a creepy feeling that wasn't a physical one, and he got both a sense of an otherworld that was hot and unpleasant and also one of an unappeasable hunger, an appetite that intended to consume him also, as soon as it was done consuming this other delicious morsel first . . .

. . . *But I catch him now . . . since he close to me . . . Yes, not wait! Right now!*

Bob leapt away from the bathtub just in time, split seconds after the warning impressions flashed through his mind.

Back at the safety of the bathroom door, he saw how narrow his escape had been. Focused on secreting the cellphone into Amanda's waistband, he'd not noticed the baby reaching for him with its long bloody fingers curled in readiness to encircle his neck.

On realizing its trap had failed, the demon baby seemingly lost interest in Bob again and returned its attention to Amanda.

Although trembling from the knowledge of how close to being killed and eaten he'd just come, Bob nonetheless insisted on remaining by the door to ensure the baby ate up all the evidence.

Amanda's hips, cellphone and all included, were shortly on their way into the baby's unnaturally capacious stomach, and when it began eating her legs, her left heel was pulled away from stopping the drain and most of the backed-up blood drained away.

And then Amanda was all gone too, and the demon baby was licking up the remaining blood in the bathtub with its warty tongue, while at the same time reaching out of it and picking up the scraps of regurgitated and rotted meat that dotted the bathroom floor. It ate the maggots feeding on the meat too.

Satisfied that there was no longer any evidence to connect him to Amanda's death, Bob shut the bathroom door and locked it. He felt it was best to quit while he was ahead, to get out while getting out was still an option, before the demon baby tried to revisit its plan of eating him too.

CHAPTER 38

Bob sat in his living room in a numbed state. Now that the adrenalin rush of what had just transpired in the bathroom was past, shock was settling in and his mind appeared to be shutting down on him. But he couldn't let it.

A short while ago, Amanda was here; alive and well . . . Now she's gone, never to be seen again. . . . Maryanne's gone too . . . for good. No evidence connects me to her disappearance anymore. Blood . . . blood. Blue baby's licked that all up . . . And from the way it's going, all of the maggoty meat that had spilled onto the bathroom floor will surely soon vanish too, down into baby's belly. . . What do I do about baby? That's the huge problem now. I still have a lot of meat in the fridge and I'll have to shop for more. But for how long? I need to get rid of that thing soon or it'll soon get rid of me!

To settle his thoughts and navigate the waves of shock flooding him, Bob watched TV for a while. But he couldn't concentrate on any of the sports programs that he tuned the TV to. He kept seeing Amanda's face as she struggled to escape from the blue hands that had killed her.

No, no. Amanda was a good person. She didn't deserve that. It would be cold and callous of me to think that what's done is done, and be glad I'm now in the clear.

The shock Bob was experiencing slowly wore off, but his thoughts continued in this gloomy vein until they were interrupted by the sound of a car pulling into the parking lot downstairs.

He walked over to the drapes and parted them. Ashley had just arrived home from somewhere. Bob watched her park, retrieve a grocery bag from the passenger-side front seat, and then get out and lock her car. He watched her cross the parking lot, and once she passed out of view, he pulled the drapes closed again and went to sit down.

He gazed at the TV without seeing anything. He heard the sound of the elevator rising to the third floor and frowned.

It's about damn time I renegotiate my deal with Ashley, he decided. *She's gonna be in for a real shock.*

He went to have a bath and change his clothes.

When Bob stepped out of his condo to go visit Ashley, it occurred to him that he'd forgotten something.

When did Rodney say he'd be back to watch the game? Was it today or tomorrow? So much has happened today that I no longer remember.

Try hard as he might, Bob couldn't remember when Rodney was due to come upstairs, so he got out his cellphone and called Rodney. But when Rodney's phone kept going to voicemail, Bob left him a voice message instead, saying he had to step out for a while (he had no intention of letting Rodney know he was going to meet Ashley) and that he'd leave the spare key under the doormat for him.

Once Bob had gotten the spare key from inside the condo and placed it under the doormat for Rodney to retrieve, he climbed the stairs to go have what he hoped would be his 'Emancipation Proclamation' with Ashley.

This was after all America, and slavery was illegal nowadays.

CHAPTER 39

"Again?" was the first thing Ashley said after Bob told her he wanted out of their relationship.

Ashley was not amused. She stood there in her hot pants and short tee shirt which showed off her body to best advantage and scowled at him in rising irritation.

"What sort of a wimpy boyfriend are you anyway?" she asked.

"One of convenience," he replied calmly. Bob felt he had the upper hand here, and refused to be cowed. "Listen, I'm fine with dating you and all, but if you keep torturing me the way you're doing, I'll be dead before the end of the week."

She gave an exasperated sigh like her anger balloon had deflated, and her shoulders slumped. "No, you won't die. I know what I'm doing."

"And I, darling, know exactly how terrible I feel while you're doing it to me." He looked her straight in the face, not flinching from her displeased gaze. "We've been lovers for what—two days? And already I've been striped like a zebra and electrocuted for crimes of passion."

Ashley grinned. "I like how you put that."

"Put what?"

" 'Electrocuted for crimes of passion.' I never thought of it that way. I viewed what we did as 'shock therapy' that makes my little Bobby a better-behaved slave. You are my slave, remember? That was our agreement."

Bob rolled his eyes. "Don't you get it? You can't keep hurting me just because you're helping me. Think of something else to accept as payment. There's always money. You can even have my condo—it's half-paid for. I'll keep up the payments and you can sell it to whoever you like."

"No. I already made it plain to you that I'm not a materialistic woman. I want to own your body . . . and your soul if you'll surrender it to me too."

Thinking she must be mad to make such a suggestion, Bob angrily asked, "What use would my soul be to you, Ashley? Do you worship the devil too? I thought that was your mom's schtick."

Ashley walked over and sat next to him. "Don't be nasty, darling." She reached out a hand and traced her fingers along the angle of his jaw. "You want me to keep helping you, don't you?"

"This is simply blackmail."

"Answer my question. Do you still want my help?"

"Maybe not. After all, there's no longer any evidence connecting me to the crime."

Ashley shook her head at him. "Darling, I don't believe you're that naïve. If I buried the evidence, can't I dig it up again? Remember, Bobby, that I know where the body is buried."

Oh no, you don't, baby. Not anymore, Bob thought with a cold smile.

But Ashley wasn't done speaking:

"All it would take to implicate you to the cops," she went on, "would be an anonymous email to them, explaining that your wife Maryanne is actually dead, not down in Venezuela, like everyone now believes; along with video attachments that proved I faked everything. To further implicate you, I'll include recordings I made of our conversations."

Bob felt sure she was bluffing about recording their conversations. He decided to call her bluff. "If you implicate me, you'll implicate yourself too."

"I'm a woman. I'll plead vulnerability. My lawyers will argue that you threatened to kill me just like you did Maryanne. I'll tell them you murdered Maryanne because you were stalking me, and then . . . I think you get the picture."

"You're crazy. None of that ever happened. I never stalked you. I don't even really like you. I hate you."

"Stop with the hatred nonsense. You love me like you love your own mother. You love me more actually, because you can fuck me and you can't fuck her."

"Ashley, please leave my mother out of this."

She grinned at him. "But, baby, it's the truth, the whole fucking truth, and nothing but the truth. That's the attraction of every wife, and why mama always loses out in the end. You sucked mama's breasts for maybe two years tops, but you'll be sucking your wife's breasts for maybe forty years, both before, during, and after she's breastfeeding your children. See? There's no competition; none at all."

Ashley leaned forward and kissed Bob on the lips. "So don't screw me over and I won't screw you over either. We need each other like a mortician needs corpses."

Shit, Bob thought as the chilling realization hit him that Ashley was right. *The spider still has the fly in her web.*

The previously indignant expression on Bob's face turned to one of distressed acceptance of his fate. On seeing this, Ashley pulled her skimpy tee shirt off over her head so that her breasts were on display. "You know what your problem is? I think you're stressed out. And that's something I can fix for you, my little slave. Come into the bedroom; I'll calm you down with a blowjob."

"No."

"I'm ordering you to take off your pants and let me fellate your penis."

Bob shook his head. "I'm not disobeying you. I'm just so stressed I'll never get hard. I've had a real rough day."

"What kind of a rough day?" Ashley asked sarcastically. "Did you accidently kill someone else?"

Remembering the demon baby downstairs in his bathroom and what it had done to Amanda Fenton a short while ago, Bob had to laugh at that question. "Trust me, darling—I mean 'mistress,' you'd never believe me if I tell you what happened to me today. But it's true; at the moment I'm in no mood for sex. It's nothing to do with you. You're still as gorgeous as you were yesterday."

Ashley stared hard at him, then decided he wasn't lying. "Okay, I'll get us both some wine to relax us."

Bob raised questioning eyebrows. "Drugged wine again, mistress?"

"That's for me to know and you to dread."

At that moment, Bob could have said 'fuck it all,' gotten up, and left Ashley's condo. Just called her bluff and taken his chances.

But he didn't. At the present, inertia seemed a better choice to him than action, since doing things only appeared to lead him to more trouble.

I'm surfing waves from crisis to crisis. If I surf left, there's corpses and demonic infants, and if I surf right there's the police and a guaranteed murder conviction. And if I don't do either, if I just ride the wave to shore . . . there's Ashley.

Ashley returned with two glasses and a bottle of pale wine.

"I haven't even shared Maryanne's latest update from Venezuela with you yet," Ashley said, placing the glasses on the end table by Bob's elbow.

"Oh yeah?" Bob asked in a state of inexplicable calm. "What did she say?"

"Check your cellphone. I uploaded it just before you got here."

While Ashley poured out their wine, Bob checked the fictional Maryanne's latest post.

In this post Mario's face was unveiled. The imaginary young man looked suspiciously like a young Fidel Castro; but no one in this present day and age was likely to make that connection.

There were three pictures: Two in which 'Maryanne' and Mario were kissing near Caracas landmarks, and a third, everyday 'girlfriend and boyfriend' picture, where the couple sat holding hands on a couch. Then there was a 'selfie video' taken by Maryanne of herself as a passenger in a car, leaning against Mario and making the victory sign while he drove through the city.

Bob felt chilled by how realistic it all seemed. Now that Maryanne's body had vanished from downstairs, he could almost believe himself that she really was alive and well two thousand miles away; and sucking some macho Latino's penis every night.

The message accompanying Maryanne's post read: "I'm sorry, guys, but I'm not gonna be making any more posts for a while. Mario and I are maintaining radio silence 'cos I don't want my controlling ex—MEANING YOU, BOB—tracking me and my darling down via our cellphones. It's sad that in this supposedly enlightened and feminist liberated day and age, a woman still has no real protection from brutal and controlling men. She isn't safe even after leaving such a person. So, please, people, don't give any of my contact information to Bob or any of his friends.

"Sorry, Linda, but I won't be able to be a bridesmaid at your wedding like we planned.

"Mario and I will come back online when it's safe for us to do so; when we're sure there's no further threat to our lives from the man I once loved and thought was a good, kindhearted person. Just shows you how wrong a judge of character one can be in affairs of the heart."

Under the post a rash of comments had already started, with most commentors offering support and sympathy.

One commentor called Bob 'a real waste of human skin." Another, a woman, said she'd always been suspicious of those 'supposedly nice types,' adding that it was better to marry a 'bad boy' because then it was all out in the open; and anyway, it was well known that 'bad boys' had bigger d*cks anyway than wimpy nice guys.

A male commentor wished Bob 'All the cancer in the world for Christmas,' while someone else called for stricter legislation restraining spouses from stalking one another, and suggested the US Senate seek to extend the jurisdiction in such cases to cover cases of such nature that occurred outside of American soil. At least three commentors posted memes of Bob as a serial killer.

"But this is absolute trash," Bob said angrily and stopped reading through the thread of comments, a thread that was lengthening by the moment, as more comments poured in. "I never treated Maryanne—"

Then he realized he'd gotten sucked into the illusion too.

"I'm good, huh?" Ashley asked, with a pleased smile on her face.

He nodded back at her. "You're seriously fantastic," he replied. "It's just too bad . . ."

She smiled coolly. "Too bad I'm a sexual pervert?"

"Well, I guess one can't have everything one wants. Say, you know you've got fantastic tits?"

Ashley laughed and handed him a glass of wine. "Drink up, baby. You've no idea in the world what I've got planned for both 'Maryanne' and yourself next. You'll love me for real after that."

Bob, damned if he did, and similarly damned if he didn't, accepted the glass of wine from her and drank deeply.

Of course, the wine was drugged. Soon Bob felt the peculiar drowsiness and dread apprehension stealing over him again. And after that he was once more unconscious and helpless.

CHAPTER 40

Funny how people love each other until suddenly they don't love each other anymore, Rodney Sherrick thought as he rode the elevator up to the second floor. His mind was full of Maryanne's posts from Venezuela in which she'd broken up with his friend Bob and then signed off from social media for a while.

Rodney still couldn't believe what was happening to his two friends.

They seemed like such a happy couple. But then, so did mom and dad.

Rodney had personal experience of this sort of thing. After twenty-four years of marriage, his mom Francine had woken up one morning, called his dad Mickey a "broke-ass punk who'd never amounted to anything in his damn life," packed up all of her belongings, and moved out of their home.

Nothing that Rodney's dad Mickey or Rodney and his older two sisters could say could make Francine change her mind. She was done with her 'no-good husband' and that was that. That had been six years ago and neither his mother nor father had remarried since. And neither of them seemed happy apart either. His mother still lived alone after all that time, while his dad spent most of his paycheck on booze and hookers.

I guess you simply love people until you don't love them anymore, Rodney thought, shifting his load of beer from one hand to the other as the elevator stopped on Bob's floor. *And you don't actually need a good reason to stop loving someone. Almost anything will do, lack of money, ill-treatment, kids. Even . . . lack of kids.*

In hindsight, it seemed to Rodney that his mother had left his father simply because, with their kids grown up and out of their home, she had nothing more to do and nothing more to talk about; as if the children had been the glue holding the marriage together.

But in mom and dad's case they were married for over two decades before things turned sour between them. Bob and Maryanne have been married for how long? Two and a half years?

Rodney couldn't understand why Maryanne had suddenly deserted what seemed to him a blissfully happy marriage. It made no sense to him.

He stepped out of the elevator. Taking the elevator up a single floor always embarrassed him, but he was a fat guy and sometimes even the shortest walks tired him out. In addition to a couple of six packs of beer, Rodney had also brought along some hamburgers and two comedy DVDs, which he thought might help Bob's mood. Their original plan had been to watch a basketball game, but Rodney doubted if, considering what was going on in his life, Bob would be in the mood for sports now.

He walked to Bob's front door and got the key out from under the doormat.

He opened the door, stepped inside, and frowning, walked through to the kitchen.

As a man who didn't currently have a girlfriend, Rodney Sherrick could immediately sense the difference between Bob's home and his own bachelor condo. This place had a woman's touch; inside of it you got that special feeling of completeness, of Ying and Yang in harmony; both sexes synchronized like they were meant to be.

Not like his own place that shrieked of testosterone overload. No female fragrance down there, no feminine traces anywhere. Just glaring masculinity on display.

Rodney figured it was time he found a girlfriend again.

I'm real tired of everyone suggesting I'm gay. Soon those gay guys at the corner deli are gonna assume it's true and start hitting on me. I keep meeting pretty women at the video store, and some of them really like me. But . . .

But Rodney was wary of ending up like his parents had.

I don't wanna invest all of that time and energy into a relationship . . . into a woman . . . only to wake up one day and find it was all a pipedream. Five years together and just bad memories to show for it. Nah, not me. I've already had some of that experience with Brooke. Once bitten, thrice shy.

On opening up Bob's fridge so he could put in the beers to cool down, Rodney stopped and stared at the fridge's contents.

Speaking of bitten, why's Bob got so much meat in the fridge if he and Maryanne were leaving town? Has to be at least twenty kilos of beef in here. He laughed. *If I didn't know Maryanne was holidaying down in Venezuela with that jerk, I'd think Bob had murdered her and chopped her up and planned to eat her to hide the evidence!*

Rodney laughed at such a silly thought. It was a joke he could tell Bob later; but only when Bob was in better spirits.

Rodney shifted the meat aside and made space for the beers. He took one beer out of a six pack, and looked around for a tray to place the burgers on.

The kitchen's spic and span beauty dazzled him. It also filled him with a sense of loss and nostalgia. This was exactly how the kitchen in their house had always looked when his mom had been around.

After she left, not at all. Rodney's sisters were both already married by then, and he too was already living away from home, so it had fallen to their father to keep house for himself. The difference had been obvious every single time that Rodney visited. At first his dad had tried his best to carry on as if nothing had changed, but he soon let both himself and the house go.

Soon the old man's kitchen was as much a mess as Rodney's now was downstairs, with everything all over the place, and only the barest modicum of an attempt made to be clean and tidy.

Rodney located his tray, pushed away the bad memories, and returned to the living room

Where'd Bob go anyway? Hopefully not to hang himself, 'cos I know how much he loves Maryanne!

This grim thought refused to leave Rodney's mind until the basketball game started and sucked him in. Rodney drank and watched and waited for Bob to return home.

CHAPTER 41

Bob awoke in the familiar room, but once more in a different situation.

This time he wasn't chained to either of Ashley's X-Frames. Instead, he was bound to a chair he was sitting on, with his hands tied behind him and each ankle shackled to one of the chair's front pair of legs. A final strap bound his waist to the back of the chair. Though comfortable, having a padded leather seat and backrest, the chair was a sturdy one, and one obviously designed for shackling people; behind him, Bob could feel the metal loop to which the straps securing his wrists were connected, and looking down revealed that the chair's metal legs all resided in depressions in the floor, which meant it couldn't be shifted from its position.

This last observation was however one that Bob only made later on. Because he'd woken up this time to the feeling of Ashley masturbating him.

Ashley was kneeling between his legs and was working on his penis, which, in response to the pleasant manipulation, was already half-erect. Soon he was fully erect and now he noticed that, tonight also, Ashley had slipped a cock-ring around the base of his penis and testicles before working on it. He clearly wasn't about to be electrocuted again, however, as this penis-ring was made of thick rubber instead of metal; it looked like a donut wrapped around the base of his genitals.

Ashley looked up at his face and grinned. "Hi, darling. Glad you're awake again." She resumed jerking on his penis until the long thick vein on its topside bulged fat with blood.

Once again, the gag-ball in Bob's mouth prevented him from replying her. If she hadn't gagged him, he'd have been pleading with her to free him, because the close attention she was playing to his penis meant she had bad plans for it. Once more, she'd trained her video cameras on Bob's plight.

Ashley rose to her feet and stepped back, to a point where they each could fully see one another. She was completely naked; but her physical beauty seemed wasted, as he'd not gotten to make love to her yet. "Earlier, you said you were too stressed out to get an erection." She pointed beside him, to an empty hypodermic syringe lying on the floor. "I've taken care of that for us. I gave you a cocktail of drugs that'll keep you hard for hours and hours. We'll have lots of fun."

That sounded really bad to Bob.

And then it got worse. Bob almost shat himself when Ashley picked up the stapler.

Waving the shiny office tool in Bob's face, Ashley told him. "I've wanted to do this to someone ever since I read that one of the Wachowski sisters—you know the two trans ladies who filmed the Matrix films—well, I read somewhere that one of them was dating a dominatrix who'd once stuck three hundred needles in a guy's cock."

Bob's eyes instantly bulged out with fright. *Hell no, she's crazy! She can't be serious!*

Ashley stepped towards him. "So, fast-forward to us now. I'm not sure we can get three hundred staples into your dick, baby, but let's try our best, shall we? I'm thinking that because, unlike a needle, each staple has two points, we should be able to make it to at least a hundred and fifty before we run out of space."

CHAPTER 42

After drinking two more beers and eating his burger, Rodney needed to pee. The basketball game was at half-time now. If he didn't drain the lizard now, he'd need to wait till the end of the third quarter to use the bathroom.

Wondering why Bob was taking so long to get back home, Rodney got to his feet and shambled into the hallway, enroute to the guest bathroom.

The beers were working a little on Rodney's mind now, and he was coming up with a plan to do something for Bob.

Rodney Sherrick knew some people in Venezuela, some filmmakers he'd met at an indy film convention in New York a year ago. He and his cousin Rudy were helping the Venezuelan guys distribute their films in the USA through their video outlets.

So, Rodney didn't think it'd be difficult to ask his friends to check on Maryanne and see what the hell was going on with her. Nothing too intrusive, however. He just wanted to be sure that Maryanne wasn't being taken advantage of by some fickle playboy who'd just use her and dump her, or worse yet, would use her to mule cocaine back home to the USA.

Sure, now we're playing cops and robbers.

Rodney laughed. The plan seemed outrageous to him. International spy shit. He didn't think it would count as stalking though, since he and not Bob would be the one handling things, but he didn't know how Bob would like the suggestion.

I know he really loves Maryanne. So just knowing that she's happy and not in any danger should cheer him up a little. Nah, I'm being dumb. Knowing she's happily having sex with that Mario guy isn't going to cheer him up. I know better. I remember how dad behaved after mom deserted us . . . No, no, no . . . she didn't desert US—we'd all already left home, like we'd deserted mom and dad. So, mom just left dad. And afterwards, when we'd visit the house, dad would look like he'd been crying when we weren't there. Anyhow, I'll run the idea by Bob and see what he says. If he acts too crazy at the suggestion, I'll say I was just joking and to forget it.

Rodney tried to open up the bathroom door, but though the handle twisted, it wouldn't open. It took him a little while to work out that the door was locked. Which puzzled him, as it hadn't happened before. The key was in the lock however, so no harm was done to his need to empty his bladder.

Wow, what a nasty smell, was his next thought, when he stepped inside the bathroom. The bathroom itself was clean, but stank like . . .

Like raw meat . . . ? This too didn't make any sense to Rodney, who now began feeling uneasy, because he remembered all the raw meat he'd earlier noticed in Bob's fridge.

Stop being silly, Rodney cautioned himself. *Bob did not butcher Maryanne in here and stock her in his fridge! This is real life, you idiot. You're being influenced by all of those crazy films you keep watching. There's a burst pipe somewhere in the building, and the smell of it is backing up through the drains in here. Bob must've locked the bathroom door because he needs to get a plumber in here.*

The bathroom window was shut, locking the nasty smell in, which was possibly why the smell oppressed Rodney so much. He quickly walked over to the window and opened it up. He relaxed as gusts of fresh night air blew into the room.

He grinned to himself. *Yeah, I do need to stop being so impressionable. Those packs of meat in Bob's fridge all clearly showed the brand name of the grocery store. What will I imagine next?*

To further freshen up the air in the bathroom, Rodney grabbed an aerosol can standing on the washstand and liberally sprayed the place.

There, it's all okay now. Alright, I gotta pee!

He could hear the TV out in the living room. Halftime was almost over. Time to return to the basketball game.

So, Rodney gave the toilet his full attention now. He unzipped his pants and lifted up both the toilet seat cover and the toilet seat, which were down.

Then he stared in horror down into the toilet bowl.

There was something blue in there and whatever it was, was very alive. Bob took a few steps back and hastily zipped up again. He was unable to take his eyes off of the blue creature that was now quickly clambering out of the toilet.

The creature looked like a goblin of some kind and seemed about two feet tall. A bright blue goblin, with a massive head, long arms, short legs and a mouth full of teeth.

Food! The word echoed in Rodney's mind like a synthesizer bass note washed in reverb. *Food!*

The blue creature was perched on the rim of the toilet bowl now. As Rodney hastily backpedaled to get away from it, it leapt at him.

Howling in fright, Rodney leapt for the bathroom door. He almost reached the door, but suddenly the little blue monster had a hold of him, and its mouth was open and it was snapping at him and trying to bite him. In a panic he staggered across the bathroom, almost falling into the bathtub in his desperation to get away from this inexplicable horror.

Rodney finally succeeded in knocking the little goblin thing to the floor, but this proved to be his undoing.

Holding onto the door to steady himself, he kicked at the blue creature. But he either mistimed his kick or the thing had understood what he intended to do, because the next thing Rodney knew was, his entire right foot was swallowed up in the thing's mouth and it was chomping down on his leg.

He endured a moment's blinding pain, and then the blue thing had bitten off his entire right foot. The little monster chewed and swallowed his foot; complete with his shoe and accompanying trouser cuff.

Rodney stared down at the bloody stump that remained of his right leg, and which was now squirting blood onto the bathroom floor.

Whimpering from the agony, and still uncomprehending what was going on, Rodney Sherrick hopped backward on his remaining leg; now attempting to make it out into the hallway, and then save himself by locking the creature in the bathroom.

His plan might have worked, but he was on the wrong side of the bathroom door, and so his backward motion served to knock the door shut instead. By the time Rodney realized his mistake and tried to get the bathroom door open again, the blue goblin thing was climbing up his body.

His attempt to swat it away proved counterproductive and ending in Rodney losing his right arm also, bitten off up to the elbow when it entered the creature's mouth.

Next, Rodney slipped in his own spilled blood and lost his grip on the bathroom door altogether. He landed on his ass on the bloody floor.

Now, weakened by the blood he'd lost, he was no match at all for the little blue monster when it leapt up onto his shoulder and enclosed his entire head in its outsized mouth.

Rodney Sherrick saw the blue interior of the blue goblin's mouth for a brief moment, and then felt excruciating pain as the monster bit his head off.

CHAPTER 43

Ashley stapled Bob in the dick and Bob bit down hard on the gag-ball. The pain of the stapling made him close his eyes. Then he opened them and looked down at his penis. The silver staple was stuck in his flesh, halfway along the side of his erection. He watched a little bead of blood well up at each of its ends.

"Alright, that's number one in. Let's try for number two, shall we?"

No, no, NO, you crazy bitch! Bob mentally shrieked at her, and tried to haul himself out of the chair. But the chair remained solidly locked to the floor. And the straps around his waist meant he couldn't even move his hips out of the way.

She stapled him again, this time on the other side of his penis. More pain, more blood, and another muffled scream from Bob. The stapler was regular-sized, meaning the staples were small, but the pain they caused the sufferer was completely out of proportion to their littleness.

"So, that's two." Ashley grinned at Bob. "Let's go on, shall we?"

He shook his head at her. "Mmmph! Mmmph!"

"No . . . no? Of course, you don't really mean that. You're just being bashful 'cos you're on sex-tape. C'mon, hon, our fun has just begun."

She now began stapling Bob's penis in a methodical way, while he screamed into the gag, bit down on it, and tears welled up in his eyes, though he determined not to burst out crying. But the agony he was feeling couldn't be quantified in words. His cock, oh, his poor bleeding cock. He trembled, and shivered and wanted to die, while Ashley continued stapling his penis in a straight line from root to tip, though she didn't put any staples into his glans yet. He closed his eyes, bit down into the gag-ball, and tried unsuccessfully to mentally separate himself from the pain like mystics did.

"Now that's great," Ashley said after a while. "Have a look, Bobby."

Before she'd spoken, Bob had felt like he was slipping away into unconscious again, which would have been a blessing from heaven.

But he was jerked fully awake by a slap in the face. "I said look at your penis, slave. See what I've written on it."

Written on it? Bob looked down and saw that Ashley had stapled 'BOB LUVS ASHLEY' along the right side of his penis, right below the fat top vein which she'd so far not touched, maybe because of the risk of uncontrollable bleeding. The metal words were distorted and bloody, but she'd shaped them correctly and made them easy to read.

Bob stared up at her in horror. She giggled down at him. "And you know what I'm gonna write next, honey-pie?"

"HMMMPH! HMMPH!"

"Let you go?" She wagged the bloody stapler at him. "Not yet, darling. I'll tell you what I'm gonna write next on your lovely fat cock. I'm gonna write 'Ashley loves Bob too!' "

And that's what she did, this time working along the left side of his erection. Bob began weeping then. He simply couldn't hold back the tears anymore.

When the unbearable torment ceased, Bob looked down at his penis, which was again decorated with another line of silver capital letters. He stared at his tormentor in horror, wondering why the pain hadn't yet caused him to go limp. Even with the cock-ring in place, maintaining an erection under these conditions seemed impossible.

Ashley seemed to read his thoughts and she giggled. She gestured again at her discarded syringe. "I already told you—the stuff I injected you with is special, I got it from a friend of my mom's named Miriam Heller. You'll stay hard even if I cut the head of your dick off." She winked at him. "Should we try that out and see if it's true?"

Bob desperately shook his head. "Mmmph! Mmmph!"

"I didn't think it'd be a good idea either. But I might change my mind and cut you, if you don't make me come now."

Bob gaped at her and then gaped down at his penis.

Come? What the hell is she talking about?

"Now let's fuck." Ashley said, dropping the stapler on the floor. "You're my man, honey. I mustn't deny you my tender, sweet, wet pussy."

And that said, she stepped forward and straddled him, sliding down her dripping vagina over his metal-studded and bleeding penis.

She rode him, and Bob really began weeping then. He felt no pleasure at all, just tremors of pain. Each time she rammed her crotch down on his, it felt like all those metal staples were stabbing into him again. The tears rolled down his cheeks, and she rubbed her breasts in the tears, laughing in delight at the effect she was having on him, while Bob wondered how she could be so evil, and how she seemed able to increase his suffering each time they met.

I should never have asked her for her help! I was crazy to ask her for her help.

And then Ashley began shuddering in orgasm. "Oh, baby! Oh, baby!" she gasped, gripping his shoulders and then yelping as her climax claimed her.

Then she slumped against Bob and held him tight for a while.

"Oh, darling, that was so wonderful," she gasped afterwards, her sex still filled with his, while he prayed that she'd get up off him and remove the staples with which she had pierced his manhood.

But Ashley didn't get up. Instead, she smiled. "Honey, that sex was so great that I wanna go again. You didn't come just now, did you?"

She laughed at his bug-eyed stare. "Tell you what I'm gonna do. Maybe my pussy wasn't tight enough for you. So . . . this time, I'm gonna let you fuck my ass. That way you'll really feel it."

"MMMPH! HMMPH! HMMMMMMPH!"

"Don't be bashful, honey. All guys love anal. It's the un-hole-ly grail of sex."

And so, she slid up off him, and while Bob stared down at the bloody mess she'd made of his crotch, she slid back down on him again, this time diverting him into her rear passage.

"See, honey, blood is a great sexual lubricant."

Yes, she was tight back there. Excruciatingly so for a man already bleeding from over seventy staples in his penis. Each time Ashley rode either up or down on him, Bob felt like his cock was being electrocuted, burnt to cinders with a blowtorch, or cut off of his body. In fact, he wished that Ashley would simply castrate him so he didn't have to endure any more of this agony.

And after a while, Bob realized that Ashley was actually tightening her anus on his penis to hurt him further. Oh, what a wicked, evil lover she was.

It was no wonder then that he fainted before she came again.

CHAPTER 44

Bob awoke again in Ashley's bed. The lights in her bedroom were turned off. This time she was sleeping in bed beside him.

Bob was still naked. Once he remembered what he'd earlier been through in Ashley's torture chamber, his first impulse was to grab his penis. When he did so, he discovered Ashley had bandaged him up down there.

He stared over at her. She lay on her side facing him, with one leg over his, her face serene in dreamland. It struck him that the normalcy, mundanity even, of this bedroom scene belied the craziness of their relationship.

He disentangled his body from hers and then got out of bed and walked into the en suite bathroom, partly to urinate and partly to see what he looked like now. Walking made him realize that he felt a little groggy. Inside the bathroom, he shut the door and put on the light.

His penis looked like a clean white package. It felt numb in its bandage, meaning she'd rubbed an anesthetic cream on it, most likely the same one she'd applied to his welts after whipping him. Squeezing his penis carefully through its wrapping revealed no sign of metal in the organ.

Seeing as he hadn't ejaculated while she was tormenting him, how she'd gotten the cock-ring off was beyond him. Maybe she'd sliced the rubber donut away with a razor . . . a thought which made him shudder on realizing how utterly helpless he'd been in her hands.

He put two and two together; his current groggy state must be the result of Ashley injecting him with a sedative, so that he wouldn't wake up when she was pulling the staples out of his penis.

He sighed. She was careful then, just crazy.

He urinated out of the end of the bandage. There was no blood in the urine, which was a major relief.

After peeing, Bob searched the bathroom cabinets for the anesthetic Ashley had used on him, but it wasn't in there. Not that he even knew what it looked like anyway.

Turning off the bathroom light again, Bob stepped back into the bedroom and looked around for his clothes.

I'm getting the hell out of here before I kill her, he decided, which in his current frame of mind was a valid possibility. Right now it would be the simplest thing in the world for him to climb back into bed with Ashley Haskins and strangle her to death.

He couldn't find his clothes with the bedroom lights off, so he located the light switches by the bedroom door and flicked one of them on. His worry that the light might wake Ashley proved unfounded. When the light came on, she simply rolled over to face the other way.

A wall clock showed the time was 5 a.m.

His clothes were laid out on her dresser stool. On top of them was a small jar of pink cream and a handwritten note on pink paper.

The note read: "Thanks, darling, for a lovely session. You were utterly wonderful—the best ever. But I think maybe we got off to a too-intense start. Hey, let's cool things for a while, give you a chance to recover. Here's the cream. Rub it on your rod thrice a day. As well as being an anesthetic, it also has antibiotic properties, just in case you picked up some bugs from my ass. You can take Tylenol for any other discomfort. I'll have another great update on Maryanne's vacation status for us tomorrow. Love you loads!!!!!"

Bob carefully folded up the note and stuck it in his pocket. Then he got dressed. With his manhood in its current bandaged state, he didn't bother putting on his underpants. However, rather than stuffing the white boxer shorts in a pocket and taking them along with him, he looked around for a pen. Not finding any, he picked up one of Ashley's black eyebrow pencils, spread out the white boxers on the dresser stool where she'd be certain to see it, and inscribed on their rear in block capitals: "I fucking hate you, and I hate fucking you."

Feeling better after making this gesture, even if the gesture was a childish one, Bob picked up the jar of anesthetic cream and made his slow and awkward way back to his own condo.

CHAPTER 45

It wasn't until the sun was shining high in the sky later that Sunday morning that Bob got out of bed.

He walked into the bathroom to urinate. First of all, he unwrapped the bandage around his cock. His manhood was in better condition than he expected. Most of the feeling was back now, and it hurt like hell, but the only evidence of last night's torment were the multitude of dark pinpricks that dotted both sides of the organ, making it look like he'd been giving himself heroin shots in it.

If that crazy woman has AIDS, I'm so so infected now.

He urinated, rubbed the anesthetic ointment Ashley had given him on his penis, and bandaged it up again. Then he brushed his teeth and checked his emails and other cellphone notifications.

Nothing more from 'Maryanne' yet. But that was to be expected. Yesterday, she'd posted that she was maintaining radio silence for a while.

There was nothing of interest on the cellphone, except a few work emails, and a reminder from his mother to urgently call her today, which, from the number of missed calls from her in his call log, she'd sent after calling him last night with no response.

Bob quickly replied the work emails, and made a mental note to vid-call his mother around noon. The urgency of her text meant she was baffled about the unexpected breakdown of his marriage and worried about his state of mind. His mother would also want to discuss the implications of Maryanne's desertion for Linda's upcoming wedding.

Bob sighed. One lie always led to another. He expected that relatives and close friends would soon start calling also to console him over Maryanne's betrayal. It was going to be a long day.

The time was about 10 a.m. when Bob walked out into his living room.

Time to feed the beast in the bathtub, he thought glumly. *So long as it doesn't go hungry, I've got time to figure out what to do with it.*

For a brief moment he considered luring Ashley down here on some pretense and locking her in the bathroom with the blue demon baby.

And that'll be the sweet end of my bitter S and M experience! No Ashley means no more whippings, electric shocks, or staples in my dick!

He quickly forced his mind out of that avenue of reasoning. *I'm no killer. Two unintended deaths on my conscience I can just about cope with. I'm not about to intentionally feed someone to that thing. The problem now is what to do with it, how to get rid of it.*

While thinking this, Bob had been staring at his cellphone, wondering how it had gotten from the bedroom to the living room couch before he did.

Oh wow, I really wish I could just discuss this with Jennifer. Maybe I should tell her about the baby, now that Maryanne's body is no longer in the condo to give Jennifer any strange ideas as to what really happened in here. But if I'm going to do that, I'll need to first figure out a good alternate story to explain the baby's appearance. But . . . but what if Jennifer is as confused by it as I am? What if it eats her too? Then I'll have three dead women on my conscience! I really need to think this through first! Because, amongst other things, if I involve Jennifer without letting Ashley know about it first, Ashley is gonna be mad at me . . . and then Ashley might tell her mother what really happened anyway, and then Jennifer might begin blackmailing me and . . .

Bob might have continued on this train of thought until he really did phone Jennifer Haskins to come see the demon baby in his bathroom, but suddenly he noticed the empty Coors Light can on the coffee table and the burger pack on the tray, and the baseball cap on the floor. And he was holding onto his own cellphone, meaning the one lying on the couch belonged to . . .

Oops, Rodney was here last night. I completely forgot about him! But why did he leave all of his stuff here? Or is he asleep in one of the rooms?

His thoughts were interrupted by the beeping of his cellphone. A message notification had just come in. Bob glanced at its screen. It looked like Ashley's promised 'Maryanne update' from Venezuela had just arrived. Bob was immediately curious as to why the spurious Maryanne, who'd so passionately signed off the internet yesterday, was already back online this morning.

He opened up the post. He was surprised. This post wasn't directly from Maryanne, but was actually a news article from a Venezuelan paper that a mutual friend of theirs had posted to her own Facebook timeline and tagged both himself and Maryanne in. The news article was headed: 'LOVERS DIE IN FATAL CAR CRASH,' above a link that led to the newspaper's website and an English version of the full story.

Bob clicked over to the website and began reading:

". . . Last night police and paramedics in the Venezuelan capital city of Caracas were called to the site of a fatal car crash in the El Paraíso district, in which two people died. The dead have been identified as Mario Meléndez, a resident of the Venezuelan city of Los Teques, and his American girlfriend Maryanne Wilson who was visiting him."

Bob gasped in surprise. Beneath this information were displayed both Maryanne's and Mario's photographs.

Bob continued reading:

". . . Several local resident eyewitnesses mentioned hearing gunshots before the car crashed, and there are also reports of a possible exchange of gunfire between Mario Meléndez's car and another car containing two men, who were later seen departing the scene of the accident after one man got out, walked over to the crashed vehicle, and had a look inside it. These eyewitness reports support the suspicion that the incident might be gang-related, particularly since the street where the incident occurred is right next to the Cota 905 barrio, which is notorious for drug-related gang activity.

"The Caracas police are yet to confirm these details of the accident. But we have this video clip from the scene, courtesy of a witness's cellphone."

Bob played the supplied video clip, which showed a black SUV crashing into the side of a building. The video had been recorded from about a hundred yards away and also at night, so it wasn't very distinct, but anyone watching could clearly see a man in a white hoodie run into view, peek through the front window of the crashed car, and then run off again and climb into another car that quickly zoomed off.

The newspaper article continued: "When contacted, a spokesperson for the Meléndez family said they are deeply shocked by Mario and Maryanne's deaths and are currently in mourning. There is currently no information available on funeral arrangements, but our investigations reveal that Ms. Wilson was an orphan with no close living relatives, and that, as she is currently estranged from her husband in the USA, there is speculation that she will be buried here in Venezuela too, with all expenses expected to be paid by her late boyfriend's family."

Bob went back to Facebook. Condolences were already pouring in, along with comments on how, even if Mario Meléndez was a drug runner, this was really Maryanne's husband's fault, for treating her so cavalierly that she'd run off into an unsafe situation in an unsafe foreign country.

Bob was astounded. He sat down on the couch and smiled.

Ashley is a genius. She almost makes being stapled in the penis worth it.

Almost on cue, his phone rang. It was Ashley.

"How d'you like the tragic ending of the drama, baby?"

"Ashley, baby, I love you." The words had slipped out of his mouth before he could stop himself from saying them.

"I told you you'd be in love with me for real today."

"But . . . but how in the world did you make the newspaper article? It's so realistic."

She laughed. "Tricks of the trade, Bobby. It'd take too long to explain the process. But it's a safe hack. By the time the guys at the newspaper discover the article is fake and take it down, it'll be too late, the news will be everywhere. I've programmed bots to spread the news to different websites. Clickbait stuff. Each time someone clicks on the article to read it, it's gonna be emailed to everyone in their contact list."

"I'm impressed." Bob truly was impressed.

"You know what? I've still got the files open on my work laptops. Come upstairs in a little bit and I'll show you the basics of deep-faking. We can work together on my follow-up posts about Maryanne's funeral."

"I'll come upstairs only if there's no wine-drinking involved."

Ashley laughed. "Of course not. You have my word on that. I meant what I wrote in my letter. I've just been so sexually frustrated since Tony died—I mean, since Tony left me." She giggled over the line. "Oops, slip of tongue there—what I mean is that Tony is dead to me. For good, now that we've found each other. So that's why I went so hard on you. But you're a real marine, Bobby, you took everything I threw at you and came back for more. But I'll be gentle from now on. I promise"

She sounded sincere too. "Okay, I'll be upstairs in a little bit," he agreed.

Bob then remembered the little blue monster, and how he'd better tell Ashley about it. Maybe she could suggest a way to get rid of it, or maybe she'd agree with him that the smart thing to do was to talk to her mother, and see if Jennifer had a magic spell that might work in sending the creature back to hell or wherever it was originally from.

"Hey, there's something important I need to discuss with you," he added.

"Sure, honey. Have you had any breakfast yet?"

"No, I was just getting out of bed."

"I'll make us some eggs and coffee then. And then we can plan our wedding."

"Wedding?"

"Oh, Bobby, I'm only joking, of course. But now that Maryanne's gone for good, we can be together as much as we like."

There came the sound of knocking on Bob's front door then. Loud insistent knocking.

"Okay, I gotta go; someone's at the door. See you in a little while."

"Kiss, kiss. I hope it's not a pretty girl at your door. Now that you're a widower, don't get married before you see me again."

The knocking on Bob's front door was growing louder. He hung up and walked over to peek through the spyhole. He wondered who could be knocking so violently.

"Hey, Bob, open up, I know you're in there! Open the damn door, Bob!"

Oh fuck! It's Marvin! What do I do now?

It sounded like Marvin was hitting the door with a hammer. Why couldn't he just use the buzzer like a normal person? "Bob, I said . . . open the damn door!"

Bob tried not to panic. I mustn't let my nerve fail me now. Not now, when everything seems like it's finally coming to a smooth and peaceful resolution.

Before Marvin could alert others in the house with the commotion he was making, Bob opened the front door.

Marvin stood there, a hulking brute of a man. As usual he was dressed in his biker outfit, leather and studs and metal-tipped boots.

"Where's Amanda?" Marvin asked Bob in a threatening voice, with a scowl on his face that threatened to eat Bob for breakfast if he gave the wrong answer.

"I . . . I . . . I don't know where she is," Bob lied.

"Don't lie to me, Bob," Marvin said, shoving Bob out of the way as he shouldered his way into the room. "Amanda called me at work yesterday afternoon and told me she was coming here to see you."

Bob followed him in silence, wondering what to tell the guy.

Once in Bob's living room, Marvin seemed to dominate it with his massive presence. Marvin worked at 'Mean Wheels,' the new biker bar near Rudy's Truck Stop up around the Blue Star Memorial Highway.

Once more Bob found himself wondering about the attraction between the petite and lovely Amanda, and this hairy, ugly man who was now standing in his living room. Because it was obvious that Marvin was very concerned about Amanda. He was trying to hide it, but Bob could see the worry beneath the bluster.

"Okay, Bob, where the hell is she?"

Bob shrugged. "Listen, man. Believe me. Yeah, you're right, Amanda did come here yesterday." A shrewd thought came to his mind then; to play on Marvin's macho impression of his own weakness. He looked sad. "She said she'd told you about me and Maryanne breaking up."

Marvin just smirked at him. "Tough luck, bro. Broads can be like that sometimes; you just need to understand how to keep 'em in line. Take me and Amanda for instance. Amanda knows who's the boss around—" Then the big man scowled. "No, no, no . . . don't you dare sidetrack me with your wimpy life. Okay, so Amanda came to see you about Maryanne. What happened next?"

"She said she was going home to wait for you. No, no, she said she had to go buy groceries."

He quickly realized that had been the wrong thing to say. Because no sooner were the words out of his mouth when Marvin grabbed him by the tee shirt, and almost lifted him off his feet.

"Groceries!?" Marvin thundered in his face. "Think of another lie to tell me, you wimp. Amanda bought our groceries yesterday afternoon, before she came to see you. She said she wanted to comfort you a bit before she began cooking, and that she might invite you to eat dinner with us." He'd lifted Bob up so much now that Bob was standing on tip-toes. "But I got busy at work and couldn't make it home last night. So, where the hell is she!? I've been calling her number since yesterday, with no response. All I'm gettin' is friggin' voicemail."

Marvin let go of Bob, who crumpled against the back of the couch.

"Bob, it looks like you were the last person to see Amanda. You'd better talk, before I call the cops."

On hearing this, Bob relaxed a little. Marvin was an ex-con with a long record of crimes to his name. No way would he want to get the police involved in Amanda's disappearance except if he really had to, as he was sure to be a prime suspect in their investigations.

"Listen, call the cops if you want to," Bob told the man. "I'll even come with you to report her missing, and—"

But Marvin was already walking off through the house.

"Hey, where are you going?" Bob weakly protested. He tried to stop Marvin by grabbing his arm, but the big man shrugged him off like he was a baby.

"Out of my way, wimp. I'm looking for Amanda in here, that's what I'm doing." He sneered. "I've never trusted guys like you. You're all prim and proper, seemingly upright citizens who've never even got a parking ticket, and then it turns out you've got a basement full of missing kids and women you've been torturing for years." He turned back at the hallway entrance and wagged a threatening finger at Bob. "I'm warning you, bro. If I so much as find the slightest evidence in this condo that Amanda didn't leave here yesterday like you say she did, or that you've hurt her in some way, you're a dead fish."

"Okay, okay, look around," Bob agreed. "The bedrooms are that way."

"Shut up. I damn well know where the bedroom are. I've been here before, remember?"

Marvin stalked off, and Bob followed. Bob's one concern now was how to stop Marvin from opening up the door behind which the demon baby lurked. Sure, Marvin was a big guy, but Bob doubted he'd be any match for the creature's sharp teeth and ravenous appetite.

But if Bob was going to prevent Marvin from sharing the same fate as his girlfriend had, he was going to have to act fast. Far from conducting the slow and methodical search Bob had expected, Marvin was looking through the rooms with the fast and expert eye of a criminal who knew exactly where were the most likely places an abducted person might be stashed. He walked into Bob's bedroom, flung open the closet doors, peeked under the bed and then into the bathroom, and walked out of there and into the next room.

"Where the hell is she?"

"I'm telling you she isn't here. What do you think, that she'd leave you for a wimp like me?"

That comment cracked Marvin up with mocking laughter, but didn't stop him searching.

One thing Marvin's search quickly established, however, was that Rodney Sherrick wasn't anywhere in the house. Bob hoped this was because his friend had drunkenly wandered off home last night, forgetting his cellphone and baseball cap in the process. Bob really hoped that this was the case, because the alternative was too horrible to consider.

Before Bob knew what was happening, the next place Marvin would be searching was the guest bathroom.

"Hey, I don't think you wanna go in there," Bob said, tugging on Marvin's brawny arm to dissuade him from opening the bathroom door. "It smells like shit in there. I think a pipe's broken."

Marvin once more shrugged him off. "You know, that's exactly what I would say too, if I was hiding a captive woman in there." He turned the door handle and stepped inside the bathroom.

Bob didn't follow him. He waited to hear Marvin start screaming. He thought of simply slamming the door on Marvin, locking it, and waiting till the demon baby was done eating him. But he couldn't do it. He felt too bad about Amanda's death; even though he disliked Marvin for his bullying ways, he really didn't want him to share the same fate.

"Hey, get out of there, man—I'm telling you it's unsafe in there."

But Marvin wasn't coming out. Fearing the worst on getting no reply, Bob peeked into the bathroom, and then he relaxed a bit. Marvin wasn't dead. He was simply urinating in the toilet.

So, where the hell is the evil baby? Bob wondered. *Where the hell did the evil thing go?*

Then he noticed the open window. Wondering how the bathroom window had gotten open again after he'd earlier shut and latched it, he walked over to look at it. The fact that the window was now open filled him with fresh worries about the demon baby's whereabouts.

Oops—I think it's gotten out of the house.

He looked out of the window, saw no sign of the little blue monster anywhere, and turned back to Marvin.

"Are you satisfied now that Amanda isn't in here?" he asked the larger man.

Marvin had meanwhile finished relieving himself. But after flushing, instead of turning back to reply, he leaned over the toilet bowl and seemed to be reaching for something down behind it.

Oh, God, please, don't let the demon baby be down there, Bob silently prayed, because he couldn't see exactly what Marvin was looking at. *Please, please, God, I've enough deaths on my conscience already. Yeah, this guy's an asshole and probably deserves to die for some things he's done, but please not today and not here, God.*

But when Marvin straightened out, he was holding Bob's gun.

"This yours?" he asked, holding the firearm out to Bob.

"Yeah," Bob said, taking it from him. Oh, so that's where it had fallen when the demon baby had flung him off of it.

Marvin looked from Bob to the gun and back again. "How the hell did it get down there behind the crapper?"

"You wouldn't belie—" Bob began saying, but then changed his reply. "Hey, man, do you believe me now, that I'm not hiding Amanda in here?"

Marvin gave him a cold hard stare and then nodded. "Alright, so maybe you didn't have anything to do with her disappearance. But I'm warning you, Bob . . ."

Bob just nodded at the implied threat. "Hey, man, as you very well know, I'm having a really bad day today, and I don't need any more aggravation. My dumb wife just ran off with another guy. Now, I know you're concerned about Amanda, and I am too now. But as you can see, she's not here and I think you'd better call around her friends, and if they don't know where she is, start calling the hospitals."

Marvin nodded, and now his worry showed clearly on his face. "Yeah, that's right. I hope she's not been in an accident. That would be horrible." He got out his phone from his biker jacket and glanced at its screen. "Damn, still no word from Amanda. Where the hell can she be?"

Bob gestured to the bathroom door, indicating that Marvin exit first. After he'd followed the big man outside, he made a point of locking the door behind them. Just in case the demon baby returned 'home.' He didn't want it getting loose in the house.

Seeing him do so, Marvin gave him a confused look. "Why the hell are you locking the bathroom door again, when there's nothing in there? It doesn't even smell as funky as you said."

Bob laughed. "Believe me, man, I've got a very good reason."

As he expected, Marvin just looked at him like he was crazy.

CHAPTER 46

So far this week, Ashley Haskins had been feeling great.

Where Bob imagined his life was slowly growing worse, Ashley viewed things as being on the upswing. The issue with Tony had been a real downer, and Ashley realized she had only herself to blame for what had happened between them.

But now I've got Bob, and now he really must love me. Yes, I was very hard on him, but that's done with now. From now on I'll be nicer, nothing too extreme in the torture chamber. In a short while I'll convert Bob to loving S and M as much as I do.

With those happy thoughts in mind, Ashley walked over to open up her front door so Bob could just walk in when he arrived.

I need to give him a spare key, so he can come up anytime he likes. Then she frowned. *But not just yet. I still have that 'little something' to take care of first, before Bob can have the run of this place.*

That 'little something' was revealed when Ashley opened up her fridge.

Like he was the modern-day incarnation of the biblical John the Baptist, Tony Barbosa's severed head rested on a tray on the bottom shelf of Ashley's fridge. By now she was used to the gruesome thing being there and so didn't flinch as she had at first when she'd stored the head in her fridge.

She reached around the head for a small carton of eggs and then shut the fridge door again.

Tony Barbosa's unfortunate death had occurred during a bondage session.

He and Ashley had both had too much to drink beforehand. In hindsight, conducting an S & M session while jointly under that level of intoxication was a very bad idea; but somehow, they'd both gone through with it. As a result, however, Ashley never noticed that she'd made the strap around Tony's neck too tight, so tight that he couldn't breathe. She'd left the torture chamber to pee, and by the time she'd got back, Tony had choked to death. It had been that simple.

But Ashley hadn't dared call in the police. She had been involved in another sadist-and-masochist-related death six years ago, and even though she'd been found innocent of any wrongdoing during the subsequent police investigations (she'd simply been present in the room when the woman's death occurred), Ashley had too much illegal internet stuff going on in her life right now for law enforcement to start keeping tabs on her.

And so, unwilling to explain Tony's death to the police, Ashley had chosen to get rid of his body on her own. Using some of her knives from her torture chamber, she'd cut his body up and began throwing it away in little chunks. His lungs and most of his intestines had simply vanished down the kitchen disposal. The rest of him had been tightly wrapped in garbage bags and thrown in the dumpster for collection. Each time, she'd so shattered his bones and chopped up the accompanying meat that the pulverized remains bore no resemblance to anything human. It looked more like roadkill.

All that remained now was Tony's head in her fridge. Ashley knew she should have gotten rid of his head before now, but she was sentimentally attached to Tony. She'd loved him a lot and still regretted killing him.

But now she had Bob. So out with the old and in with the new. By tomorrow evening at the latest, Tony's head would be as much a memory as the rest of him.

Ashley spooned coffee into the coffeemaker and switched it on. She got to work frying the eggs and decided to fry some strips of bacon alongside them.

The smell of the food filled the kitchen and smoke from the frying pan trailed out through the kitchen windows.

Just like she was now doing for the dead Maryanne, Ashley had laid a false trail for Tony. At the moment, he was supposedly out west in Utah, temporarily running a strip joint with a friend. She'd still been deciding how best to kill him off down there, when Bob had approached her with his request that she help him out.

So, Ashley had put her own coverup on hold, and begun work on Bob's. And it had paid massive dividends.

The S&M videos she'd shot with Bob were also of the highest quality. Her online fans couldn't get enough of them. They were raving about him and demanding for more.

Bob can't know about the website yet. Not till he's fully a convert of the darker side of loving. Shouldn't take long though; and then we'll share the proceeds, same as I did with Tony. But first of all, I need to completely erase Maryanne from the picture. I've three optional scenarios for that. I'll let Bob decide which one we'll go with.

Ashley found it amusing how people believed whatever you told them. So long as you told something to them often enough and realistically enough, they'd come to believe it over time. Maybe it had always been so, but it appeared to be even more so in these days of the internet, when everyone's attention span was so short that they had no desire to research the truth of things for themselves.

I think that's because there's simply too much stuff to sift through out there now, and if you delay to separate fact from fiction in one story, you might miss something even more exciting that's happening elsewhere. So, once a story makes sense and has a satisfactory, or at least a logical conclusion, it's good enough for the reader.

It was different in the old days, when the only lives you knew about in minute detail were those of your family and of your closest friends.

But now, when even the most intimate details of people you don't give a shit about are available literally at the tips of your fingers, with each succeeding detail— both real and imaginary—more juicy and shocking than the previous? And not just in your own hometown or state or country, but all around the globe? And one mustn't forget all of the bloggers, vloggers, YouTubers, TikTok-ers, Instagram warriors and other so-called 'influencers' who shamelessly self-promote and go out of their way to become celebrities. Everyone wants that lucrative Google AdSense money.

Also, in Ashley's experience, people preferred fiction to fact. Fiction was generally more exciting than fact. And if you could somehow work people's fears into the offered fictional package? Well, then you had a surefire winner in the clickbait wars.

For instance, in Maryanne's case, Ashley had simply played on the average traveler's worry about how unsafe and dangerous visiting a foreign country could prove to be.

She laughed as she removed the first batch of eggs from her frying pan. *I should just write scripts for Hollywood. I'd make way better money than I do hacking the internet and selling S and M erotica.*

In Maryanne's case, Ashley had already prepared a painstakingly detailed Wikipedia page concerning Maryanne and Bob Wilson's supposedly turbulent marriage and the tragic events that led up to her death in Venezuela. She laughed each time she read it, with its long list of fictional spousal abuse incidents and unsuccessful family interventions.

But then, she reasoned, she was merely contributing her own share of fables to the fountain of misinformation called the internet.

Deciding she wanted more eggs, Ashley turned away from the cooking range and opened up the fridge again. This time, before shutting the fridge door, she blew a kiss at Tony's head.

Then she shut the fridge, turned around, and saw the little blue creature which had almost fully squeezed itself in through one of her open kitchen windows.

What the hell is that? she asked herself in silent horror, placing the fresh box of eggs on the kitchen counter with trembling fingers. *It looks like a demon baby! Dammit, has mom been casting magic spells again? Dad and I cautioned her about this, after the time she materialized that giant spider into the washing machine.*

The babylike monster plopped down into the kitchen sink. Then it opened its mouth and Ashley saw how many teeth it had and how big they were.

She didn't understand how, but at the same time as the blue creature did this, an image of an overwhelming hunger was projected from it to her, with herself as the object of that hunger, although it had originally been the smell of raw bacon that had attracted the creature in here.

Not me! Ashley grabbed up a knife and flung it at the little monster. The knife hit it in the belly and sunk in deep. Black goop spurted around the wound and the blue-skinned little horror shrieked in rage and leapt at her.

Ashley flung a meat cleaver at the thing, then turned and ran for her living room. She looked back once, saw that she'd missed with the cleaver and that the monster was still coming after her, and kept going.

She made it out to her living room, but then the thing was on her back, and suddenly it was riding her down onto her expensive couch, with its hands clenched tight around her neck.

Ashley struggled to rise, but the little blue imp's grip was like iron around her throat, and she found that she could neither throw it off of her back, nor, with her face pressed into the couch fabric like it was now, could she scream for help.

In her panicked state, Ashley was certain that her mother had something to do with this little blue monster's existence, and if she could just summon her mother in here, Jennifer Haskins might be able to prevent it from killing her.

But try as she might, Ashley was unable to get a scream out. And what made this so ironic was that because she was expecting Bob, her front door was currently ajar, and any screaming she did was certain to be heard outside of her condo.

In rising despair, Ashley felt the monster biting into her back, its sharp and jagged teeth peeling away first her skin and then her flesh. She felt it bite through her ribs and eat into her lungs. Her blood ran like the wine she'd thrice served to Bob.

Ashley Haskins had never liked experiencing pain; she'd only loved dishing it out. And so, *this*—something hurting her like this—was her worst nightmare come true; the ultimate horror she'd dreaded experiencing.

She began screaming into the couch fabric, which muffled her pain as effectively as a gag-ball would have.

Mom! Mom! Where are you? Help me, I'm dying!

Slowly but surely, things began to go black for Ashley Haskins, and she bled more and more and struggled less and less, until finally she lay raw and unmoving on the couch.

CHAPTER 47

Bob knew he'd been on a rollercoaster ride of emotions this week, constantly swinging from one extreme to the other. It seemed to him as if the Fates had been using him as their ping-pong ball.

Here's another curveball they've just thrown me, he thought as he once again ascended the stairs to Ashley's condo, occasionally wincing when his bandaged penis rubbed tightly against his pants. *Now, the monster's gone; hopefully for good. It's out of my life and I no longer have to deal with it. It's someone else's problem now.*

But then he pushed open the door to Ashley's condo unit and stepped inside of a gory fantasy.

Fuck no!

He took one look at what now remained of Ashley Haskins and quickly stepped back outside again. He left the door open just a crack, so he could keep an eye on the demon baby, which was sitting on the couch and was covered in gore, as it slowly shoved Ashley's entire left leg down its throat.

Shit, now Ashley's dead too. Bob thought. *Where the hell is this madness gonna end? And when?*

He hadn't even gotten through thinking this, when the door opposite Ashley's opened and Ashley's mother Jennifer emerged from her condo, pushing her husband Chris ahead of her in his wheelchair.

"Oh hi!" Jennifer said brightly on seeing Bob.

"Hello!" he replied carefully, unsure whether or not it would be a wise thing to let Jennifer know that her daughter was dead.

He waved to Chris too. "Hey, man, how's it going?" But Chris seemed half asleep and made no attempt to reply.

Jennifer pushed Chris towards the elevator, which was on their own side of the staircase. "We were just going out to the park to enjoy the sunshine," she explained, adding, "Is my daughter in?"

But then, before Bob could reply in the negative, Jennifer left Chris's wheelchair parked at the top of the stairs and quickly walked forward to stand beside Bob.

"Wow, I'd never have expected it of you," she whispered in Bob's ear.

He looked at her in surprise. "What are you talking about?"

"I never knew that you were into kinky sex. Or is it a result of Maryanne ditching you for that hunky Venezuelan guy?" Her tone changed. "There's a news bulletin that they're both dead, you know. Gang warfare. So sad."

But Bob wasn't interested in discussing Maryanne's fictional death.

"Jennifer, what do you mean, kinky sex? What the hell are you talking about?"

She nudged him with her elbow, and lowered her voice even more. "There's no need to be bashful with me. Don't deny it. I'm talking about your S and M shows that you put on with my daughter Ashley."

Shows? "Jennifer, how d'you know about that?"

"I saw you on Ashley's S and M website. I've got a free subscription. I'm not really into that kinky stuff myself, but occasionally I have a look, to see what my daughter's up to now." Then she looked serious again. "So, what are you gonna do now? Are you gonna have Maryanne's body brought home for burial? Technically you're still her husband you know. Well, legally."

Bob nodded distractedly, because he felt as if the floor was falling out from under his feet. How many bad surprises could a single week hold for one man? The Fates' ping-pong game simile returned to haunt and taunt him.

"Yeah, I guess," he replied Jennifer. "Please let's discuss that later. I'll come to your place so you can advise me on what to do." He forced a smile. "But for the moment, please tell me a little more about Ashley's sexy website."

Jennifer looked surprised. "You mean you didn't know?" She laughed. "Oh, but I thought she'd told you. Bob, you've been Ashley's star attraction for the past few week, doing lots of things that she'd wanted to do with Tony, but which he never consented to because he thought they were too dangerous." She winced. "Staples in the dick? Major ouch. Whatever made you do that?"

"Desperation and too much wine."

Bob understood now that his desperation had made him naïve. How hadn't he connected the dots?

An S and M dungeon with four high-definition video cameras and a woman who is a hacker? Any fool would have realized she was uploading videos to a website. He corrected himself: *Yeah, any fool who didn't have his wife's corpse in the bathroom. But . . . but now, Ashley has potentially ruined me. If those videos are ever discovered by the guys at work, I'll be out of a job for life.*

He glanced back at Ashley's door, glad now that she was dead. What sort of a nasty person uploaded such extreme videos without asking for the other participant's consent?

Then he frowned. "Why are we whispering?" he asked Jennifer.

She jerked her thumb at her motionless husband. "Chris doesn't approve of people whipping each other. In his mind Ashley's still in Catholic school."

Then Jennifer frowned. "Well, I'm really sorry to hear about Maryanne's passing. I'm doing my best to feel sad about her death, but I'm finding it really hard to be sad, now that it seems like I never really knew her at all. I feel that she'd been playing me for a fool all this while. She never even so much as hinted to me that she'd fallen out of love with you. It's all so odd, the way she just left us all, like we didn't mean a thing to her. Her death reminds me of Princess Diana's. You know she died the same way. Left her husband and died in a car crash with her boyfriend. And that boyfriend of Maryanne's. I don't know if kids of your generation would ever notice this, but he looks like Fidel Castro as a young man. The likeness between them is really astoun—"

Ashley's front door burst open then and the blue-skinned demon baby rushed out at them both.

CHAPTER 48

After that, everything became complete pandemonium.

Jennifer's first reaction on seeing the blue-skinned creature coming at them was to shriek and back away towards the staircase.

However, Jennifer didn't watch where she was going. And so, once she reached the stairway, she backed right into her husband's wheelchair.

By the time she realized her error, it was too late. Both Chris and the wheelchair had rolled off down the stairs. Man and machine reached the turn in the staircase and the wheelchair slammed into the wall, pitching Chris sideways out of sight.

Jennifer shrieked at what she'd done and fainted. Thankfully, she collapsed safely on the third-floor landing and didn't roll down the steps after her husband.

That left Bob alone to handle the demon baby. He now saw that it was wounded. Someone had stuck a knife into the left side of its torso. It was bleeding and seemed to be in pain, but it kept coming nonetheless, not pausing to pull the knife out of itself.

Food! Food! its thoughts thundered at him.

Bob stared at the nasty little creature, wondering how endless its belly was. For a moment he thought the monster would attack the fainted Jennifer, but it ignored her and came after him instead.

He retreated down the stairs away from it, descending backwards to keep it in view. Meanwhile he tried to think up a plan to neutralize it.

About the only chance I've got here is to pull the knife out of its belly and stab it with it until it's dead. If it can bleed, it can most definitely die. So, I'm going to have to kill it. I'll try to cut its head off. Other than the knife, there's also the gun in my pad. But will I even make it down there alive?

Suddenly, Bob found level ground beneath his feet again and the wall against his back. He'd reached the midway landing between the floors. His descent was now blocked first by Chris's wheelchair, which lay overturned on the landing, and then, two steps further down, by the stricken man himself, with Chris lying in a pathetic position on his back over the course of about four steps, staring up and blinking like he had no idea what the hell was going on.

Meanwhile the demon baby was coming on, slowly following Bob down the stairway as if it knew he couldn't escape it and so it had no need to rush.

The only way downstairs was around the wheelchair, and so, between shooting quick glances back at the demon baby, Bob bent to move the wheelchair.

But the demon baby clearly had a hunter's instinct. The moment Bob began to straighten up the wheelchair again, the baby launched itself at him. It leapt off the middle stairs and soared through the air like a flying squirrel.

Bob did the only thing he could. Exerting his strength more than he had in years, he lifted the wheelchair up to block off the open circle of teeth that was coming to eat his face.

Purely by accident, the blue-skinned little freak landed in the seat of the upraised wheelchair.

On seeing what had happened, Bob did the first thing that occurred to him. He flung the wheelchair, with the demon baby still riding on it, all the way down the stairs. The wheelchair sailed high over its owner, and with the demon baby peering from it like a perplexed young passenger in a Big Dipper fairground ride, it crashed high into the wall down on the second floor.

The noise of the crash reverberated upward like a gunshot echoing off a range of mountains.

Bob bent over Chris to check that he was alright, then he hurried on down the stairs. His thought was to reach his condo unit and get his gun. The demon baby was still in the wheelchair, partly flattened beneath it. But it was far from dead, and was already pulling itself out from the wreckage.

Before Bob could walk past it toward his front door, the demon baby was out of the wheelchair and was staring at him. Its hunter's instinct had clearly kicked in again, and it wanted to stop Bob from escaping into his home.

Bob stared back at the evil thing. It appeared to be wary of him now, as it was more hurt than before, with a long bleeding gash in its forehead from its crash in the wheelchair. It may even have been stunned, as he received no projected thoughts of hunger from it.

But its awful mouth looked as functional as ever, and Bob knew what those horrible teeth could do if he let them get anywhere near him.

Bob realized he'd made a mistake in delaying to study the crashed wheelchair. Now that the demon baby was out of it, he didn't dare turn his back on the creature, knowing it would leap on him the moment he did. For the moment, he and the baby were locked in a deadly stalemate, and it looked like he was once more left with the single option of using the knife stuck its body to kill it.

He backed away from it towards his condo, desiring to keep a safe distance between them both.

"The hell is that damn thing?"

Bob looked up. Marvin, massive and imposing as ever, had just stepped into the hallway. To Bob's relief, Marvin was holding a pump-action shotgun.

"I heard a crash that sounded like all hell was breaking loose out here," Marvin explained, his natural criminal caution automatically making him train the shotgun on the little blue monster, which was the main thing in this scenario that he couldn't account for. (Assuming of course, that one discounted the shattered wheelchair at the bottom of the stairs. But where oddities were concerned, the little blue imp won the condominium bizarre elections by a landslide.)

"You okay?" Marvin asked Bob, not taking his eyes off of the demon baby, which was now looking from one of them to the other, like it was wondering which of them would taste better. "Bob, what the hell is this fucking thing? It looks like . . ."

"Shoot it," Bob pleaded plaintively, running back towards the staircase. "This little blue asshole killed and ate Amanda."

That was all the information and encouragement Marvin needed. A moment after Bob stepped into the safety of the stairwell again, another thunderous sound filled the corridor, one that this time resulted in a wind of blue shreds blowing past the stairwell entrance.

"That's all she wrote for you, you li'l blue sonofabitch," Bob heard Marvin say, when his ears had stopped ringing from the thunder of the shotgun blast in such close quarters.

Bob stepped out of the stairway entrance. Most of the little blue demon baby had ceased to exist. Marvin was bent over what remained of it, which was just its head, neck and shoulders, and both arms, lying in a pool of black blood. The rest of it had been blown away by the shotgun blast.

Its jaws were still moving, however, though it was clearly dying.

"What the hell is this fucking thing?" Marvin asked in a scared voice when Bob joined him. "What the hell is it?"

"Hell if I know," Bob replied him.

Marvin gave Bob a cold look. "You said it ate Amanda. When did that happen? Why didn't you say so earlier when I was at your place?"

"Look out!" Bob shouted.

Marvin's taking his eyes off of the demon baby had been a mistake. Now, launching itself up from the floor by using its arms like springs, what remained of the creature shot through the air and fastened itself on Marvin's neck.

Before Marvin could react, Bob heard the now-familiar sickening crunch of the little monster's teeth coming together through flesh and bone. Then, Marvin's head and body fell apart in different directions, the demon baby having eaten away his entire neck in a single bite.

Bob stared at Marvin's corpse as blood spurted from it and coated the demon baby's remaining body parts. The thing was still moving, but Marvin had collapsed right on top of it and it was now wedged beneath him, with no way to free itself from his bulk. Because it no longer had a stomach, Marvin's bitten-off neck was being squeezed out whole through the stump of its torso. The chunk of meat looked like solidified red toothpaste exiting a tube.

This is crazy, Bob thought, staring at the mess. *But unlike in the movies, at least I've got the evidence that I'm not lying. The monster hasn't faded away, so the police will have to belie—*

But to his horror, what remained of the demon baby *was* fading away. First, its blue body turned transparent, then that transparency popped like a bubble, and then it was all gone.

Bob couldn't believe it. He couldn't believe it at all.

This is just so unfair, he thought. *If the monster had remained, I could've explained everything. But now that it's gone . . . the police are gonna conduct a thorough investigation and everything—once they search through Ashley's computers—everything is gonna come to light.*

Had Bob been thinking more clearly, he might have realized that he had both Jennifer and Chris to corroborate the odd tale he would have to tell the police. But because too much weird stuff had happened this week and it seemed like the rain of shit would never stop, Bob simply decided it wasn't worth it.

To compound matters, Bob was suddenly certain that the demon baby had eaten up his dear friend Rodney also. Having five deaths on his conscience seemed too much of a weight to bear.

Bob decided to end it all.

Bob wondered if he should return to his home and use his own gun to end his life. After a little consideration, he decided there was no point to doing so. He had Marvin's shotgun right here. A shotgun was supposed to do a much better job of killing one than a pistol would.

And so, Bob Wilson levered Marvin's blood-smeared shotgun out from under him, placed its muzzle under his chin and, after swearing a final curse at Ashley Haskins, pulled the trigger.

The gun boomed and half of Bob's head blew off. He lay there dying on the floor, bleeding away, with the left half of his brain reduced to pulp.

But he wasn't completely dead yet, and before his brain shut off completely, he had a strange vision:

Jennifer Haskins was crouching beside him, with a frown on her face and what looked like voodoo doll in her hand. Through Bob's remaining eye, he saw that the voodoo doll seemed to have an erection.

Then Bob felt Jennifer pulling down his pants. And next, it felt like she was snipping off some of his pubic hair.

"Oh, yes, you'll be mine now," Jennifer was saying as she worked. "All mine now."

Bob Wilson died then, not understanding in the least what was going on. It merely seemed to him that Ashley's death had driven her elderly mother crazy.

CHAPTER 49

There was heat, a whole lot of heat, and it felt like Bob was once more in Ashley's torture chamber, this time being deep-fried in oil by her.

But then the agonizing temperature eased off a bit, and Bob rose through cooler and cooler stratum until finally he opened his eyes again.

One fact was immediately clear. He was still dead. Or, if he was alive, it wasn't the same sort of life he'd just gotten through living.

He wasn't in his house as he remembered it, or even in his own bed. It came to him then that he was in Jennifer Haskins house and was lying in her bedroom.

And his body. This wasn't his body as he at all remembered it. His own body had been young and agile, while this body he now found himself inhabiting was anything but. This body was older, not yet old-aged, but nearing it. And he could feel a strange thread of weakness in his limbs when he moved them.

What? Oh no. I'm in Chris Haskins's body.

But there were two differences: where Chris had been bound to his wheelchair, Bob could move his limbs easily. He sat up in bed and then lay down again. He however understood that there was a supernatural force enabling him to move Chris's stroke-paralyzed form.

The second thing was that he couldn't talk. He tried to move his lips and tongue, but no words came from them.

But as sort of compensation for that, he could sense things he previously couldn't. He suddenly understood that Jennifer Haskins had brought him back from the dead—no, that wasn't correct: she'd imprisoned his soul before he'd really had a chance to die—and that her sole, selfish reason for doing so was so that he could have sex with her, as often as she wanted it.

Bob liked the idea of having sex. He liked it a lot. But he was Jennifer's slave and he had to satisfy her. Satisfying Jennifer on a nightly basis was his new reason for living.

He also understood that Chris Haskins was still in this body too; but for these nighttime hours, Chris was fast asleep. When Chris woke up in the morning, he—Bob—would have to depart again. But his leaving wouldn't be permanent. He'd be back here again tomorrow night when Chris had once more fallen asleep. And on all succeeding nights too.

He looked down at his crotch and saw that his penis was good and hard and ready to satisfy Jennifer Haskins.

He got up and walked out into the living room.

Jennifer had been sipping gin and watching an online video on her laptop. The video showed a young blonde woman who looked very familiar to Bob, whipping a man who looked even more familiar. The man being whipped was chained to an X-Frame and didn't appear to be enjoying the lashing.

Bob tried his best to identify the sado-masochistic couple, but he didn't succeed. Their names knocked at the door of his mind, but the key of memory wouldn't turn in the lock.

Then Jennifer heard his approach and turned to look at him. "I was wondering how soon you'd wake up, darling." She got up and stroked his erection. "It's sad, but Chris really doesn't have it in him anymore—not since his stroke. But you'll fill in for him, won't you, Bob darling?"

Bob nodded and smiled.

Jennifer licked her lips and pinched her nipples. Then she strode off towards the bedroom Bob had just emerged from, saying over her shoulder:

"Now, baby, before you return to the boiling darkness in which you'll spend all your daytime hours, come back to bed and treat me to some good lovemaking."

Bob went with her and gave her what she wanted.

The End

ABOUT THE AUTHOR

Wol-vriey is Nigerian, and quite tall.

He believes there actually are things that go bump in the night.

He writes horror fiction—for adults only, please. And also some surrealist stuff.

Wol-vriey blogs at: *http://oddityfarm.wordpress.com*

WOL-VRIEY
BIZARRO AND TRANSGRESSIVE FICTION

BOSTON POSH (BUD MALONE #1)

In 2028 AD, the USA is a nation ravaged by hungry dragons and dinosaurs. In Boston, Massachusetts, private eye Bud Malone is hired to rescue a kidnapped heiress. But nothing is as it seems.

Malone works to unravel a tangled web involving Boston Chinatown, a 200-year-old woman with a 9-year-old body, white robots, a human-liver-eating psychopath, a golem, a porcelain dragon, and a snake goddess with a crush on him. There's also a woman obsessed with chicken sex. Then Malone meets Posh Lane, a gorgeous call girl who's desperate to quit her pimp.

Romantic sparks ignite between Posh and Malone, but Posh's past suddenly catches up with her in a BIG way. To save Posh, Malone agrees to run a quest for Earth's new rulers, the Forks. But, Malone has no idea that agreeing to the Fork's odd request will send him on the weirdest trip he's ever been on in his life.

BOSTON CORPSE (BUD MALONE #2)

MAGIC CAN BE MURDER! - Drag queen Lucy Tang is back in Boston, and is hell-bent on settling her vindetta against casino owner Sookie Ling. And suddenly, Bud Malone, PI, has the case of his life to resolve.

When Boston's robot police force are baffled by a mind transfer case, they come to Malone for help. The one person who can likely help Malone out here is the witch Soledad Bathory. But Soledad seems to know a lot more than she's telling him. It's a case not made easier when Malone meets Soledad's beautiful cousin, Josephine 'Slave' Bailey. Slave has her own plans for Malone, most of which involve teaching him BDSM and making him her new Master.

Oh, and Rick Rogers owes Sookie Ling a whole lot of money, a gambling debt that's going to be literally Hell to pay!

BOSTON CORPSE - Not your average detective novel!

Burning Bulb
PUBLISHING

WOL-VRIEY
BIZARRO AND TRANSGRESSIVE FICTION

BOSTON LUST (BUD MALONE #3)

"Bless it, Father, for she has sinned."

Seven murdered gay women, all their bodies completely drained of blood. All also with large parts of their bodies dissolved away like acid has been pumped into their veins.

Bud Malone has to find the female vampire preying on Boston's lesbian population.

Then Malone meets the beautiful Trudi Carmen and the case gets even more tangled. Trudi needs Malone's help in recovering a ring that's gone missing. But how in the world is one little black ring related to either the dead women or their killer?

Resolving this case will lead Malone deep into Lucy Tang's legacy –The Abstracta. And then to the city of Genesis.

Boston Lust –Just when you thought Bean Town was safe to visit again.

HELL DANCER

Six people find themselves trapped in Detention, a nightmare realm where the demonic Schoolmaster is hell-bent on reforming them . . . until they die.

Porn superstar Venus Deluxe came to Springfield, MA to party, and next found her life hanging by a thread. One wrong answer will mean her death.

Suspended BPD detective Tanya Rockford was trying to stop one kind of violence, but found a terrifying another. With her and her companion's lives hanging in the balance, it's going to take all of her courage and resourcefulness to escape this hell she's stumbled into.

Porn stud Chad Cannon has made a career from his ten-inch penis. Here in Detention, however, it's his brains that matter. He'll soon be hoping all the pot he's smoked over the years hasn't completely messed up his memory.

The three students, Sherri, Jordan, and Mike? They were all just in the wrong place at the right time. Will anyone survive Detention? The evil Schoolmaster doesn't plan on letting that happen . . . .

Burning Bulb

WOL-VRIEY
BIZARRO AND TRANSGRESSIVE FICTION

VAGINA MUNDI

Rachel Risk is a professional thief with super-strong hair that can stretch like tentacles to manipulate objects. Ashley Status has both a digitally augmented brain, and 'muscle-purses' in her arms and legs in which she stores inflatable objects—cars, guns, rocket launchers, etc.

When Raye is framed as the fall girl in a jewel robbery, the pair flee Chicago's vengeful robot gangsters and take refuge in the Hotel Bizarre, where the gorgeous 'vagina singer,' Femina, is performing for a week.

But the Hotel Bizarre is even stranger than its name suggests, and very soon Raye and Ash are involved in an deadly adventure, a struggle for survival the likes of which they'd never imagined possible with loads of deviant sex, drugs, music, and violence at every turn. And just what is the old woman in the skin desert really doing with all those cats glued to her walls?

VAGINA MUNDI—a Bizarro Hymn in praise of WOMAN!

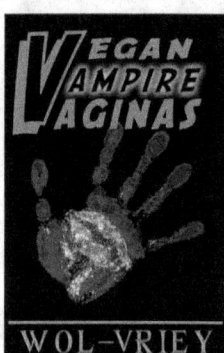

VEGAN VAMPIRE VAGINAS

The biggest bank heist in US history. And Tom Palmer can't remember pulling it off. And no, this isn't your standard case of amnesia. After a one-night-stand gone horribly wrong, Boston salesman Tom Palmer wakes up with a vagina implanted in his left hand. Then his day gets worse.

Tom is transported across space-time to a nightmare version of Boston, one where the Bizarro virus has transformed half the population into cannibals. Worst of all, Tom discovers that in this new Boston, he's the infamous gangster Pussypalm, wanted for robbing the Federal Reserve Bank of Boston a year ago. He also learns that the vagina in his hand is prophetic, i.e. it talks . . . after sex.

With 130 people left dead during his bank heist and six billion dollars missing, Tom knows he's living on borrowed time. It is in his best interests not to remember anything. Because once he does . .

Burning Bulb

WOL-VRIEY
BIZARRO AND TRANSGRESSIVE FICTION

VEGAN ZOMBIE APOCALYPSE

In the post-apocalypse worlderness, zombies rule the earth. They're allergic to meat, and brains literally make them explode. Zombies now eat blood potatoes, parasitic tubers grown in the flesh of humancows corralled in maximum security farms. Two fugitives meet in the ancient ruins of Texas. The first is Soil 15-f, a womancow who's escaped her farm a week before she's due to be killed and her blood potato crop harvested. The second fugitive is Able Kane, former head necros food technician, now sentenced to death for heresy. But Soil is no ordinary humancow.

Unknown to herself, she's the vegan zombie agricultural revolution, and the zombies desperately want her back. And the necros equally desperately want Able Kane dead. He's fled with a forbidden discovery which will reshape the world for the worse if used. And Able is just hardheaded/misguided enough to use it.

MELANIE NEMESIS CATCHPOLE

In Springfield, Massachusetts, Melanie Catchpole is hired to fetch back a magic teddy bear worth millions of dollars from a warehouse across town. Problem is, the warehouse is down in Springfield's O-Zone that totally weird sector of the city where Bizarro fell to Earth. The 'O' is a fairytale land, a place where dreams and nightmares literally live and breathe..

Worse still, the gingers—mutant cannibals—prowl the O. The gingers have already eaten everyone else Melanie's employers sent to get back the magic teddy bear.

Accompanied by the handsome but ruthless Doug Fisher (who she finds sexy but doesn't dare entrust her heart to), Melanie enters the O-Zone. Melanie and Doug are instantly caught up in an adventure they'd never have believed credible even if written as fiction . . . and Melanie's used to experiencing the very weird as the norm.

And now, additionally, there's a mystery to unravel: What does the dark, freezing-cold being called The Fixer want with Mary, the barkeep's daughter?

Burning Bulb

WOL-VRIEY
BIZARRO AND TRANSGRESSIVE FICTION

BIG TROUBLE IN LITTLE ASS

From Bizarro master storyteller Wol-vriey comes a truly weird western tale that will leave you awe-struck and on the edge of your seat...

In the town named Little Ass, tight-assed prostitute Rosa overhears a gunslinger's plans to assassinate rancher Edison Bennett. Once the badass Bennett learns of the plot, he ensures there'll be hell to pay for any attempt on his life!

Yes, it's going to take all of gunslinger Jude's shooting prowess, his eclectic collection of strange firearms, a trusty horse that requires an owners' manual, and the help of the lovely and invigorating Nell (who's EXTREMELY odd when the going gets weird), to survive the Bizarro hell that Edison Bennett unleashes in order to hold onto the land that he'd stolen from Madam Zizi.

BIZARRO 101 (A BASIC PRIMER)

Welcome to the strange place:

A collection of 37 flash fiction stories designed to introduce one to the Bizarro/New Weird Genre.

Weird, dreamy, nightmarish, absurd, sad, surreal, humorous . . . this collection of tales is all this and more.

***

"This primer is the very essence of any and all styles and types of Bizarro writing. Wol-vriey collects, distills, and bottles up these 37 tiny stories for your sensory enjoyment. This is an absolute must-read for anyone new to the genre, because it demonstrates the scope of what Bizarro is, and what it can be."
　　　　　　　　　　　　–Teresa Pollack, Bizarro commentator and blogger

Burning Bulb
PUBLISHING

WOL-VRIEY
BIZARRO AND TRANSGRESSIVE FICTION

Dr. Orgasm

Courtney Taylor is young, intelligent, beautiful, and successful. She also has a boyfriend who loves her deeply. The problem is, no matter what Courtney does, she can't climax during sex.

When Florence Rigid's communist forces destroy the city of Metaphor, Courtney and her friends Teresa, Highball, Miki, and Heather are cast into the midst of a quest to find the only person able to save the land of Innuendo—Dr. Carol Orgasm, wanted by the communists for developing the O-Pill, a wonder drug that grants women sexual ecstasy on demand.

The communists will do anything to get their hands on the O-Pill and prevent its reaching the millions of Innuendo's women. But Courtney desperately wants that pill too. And so it's now a race between Courtney and the communists to find Dr. Orgasm first.

And Courtney has no choice but to win this race. She must win it. For her own orgasm . . . and for the freedom of female sexuality everywhere.

PUSSY TRANSMISSION

Pussy Transmission were the most decadent Pop Art ensemble of the 90's. Led by the beautiful painter Isis Lynch, the trio revolutionized the art world. Then suddenly, without explanation, Pussy Transmission vanished into historical obscurity. Now, twenty years later, three women come to Lynch Place. Lily and Nina are journalists desperate to interview Isis Lynch. Raven, on the other hand, wants to find her boyfriend, who's gone missing inside Isis's house. Raven's worried—she's heard that Pussy Transmission broke up because Isis began dabbling in black magic . . . with devastating results. All three women will shortly wish they'd never left home. Particularly once the rats in Lynch Place start warning them that they're going to die . . . and Raven meets Betty Butcher, the bouncy supernatural psycho who's intent on chopping her into bits. Pussy Transmission, Baby! Just because . . .

Burning Bulb

WOL-VRIEY
BIZARRO AND TRANSGRESSIVE FICTION

GIRLS ARE NOT SMILING

Welcome To The Road Trip From Hell

Pagan is demon-possessed.

Lori is suicidal.

Britt is just terminally pissed off.

Meet three young Boston women on the run from the law, each with problems that will fuse into more than the sum of their individual parts, becoming a holocaust of sex and violence and terror, a literal rain of blood and horror and gore and evil.

And if that wasn't already bad enough, Pagan's pet demon is slowly transforming her into something both unspeakable and unholy. Truly, these girls aren't smiling.

BLUE NIGHTMARES

Consummate EVIL is coming. It is relentless and unavoidable. It is Blue.

Jessica Schreiber is seeing things. Very horrible things. Since arriving in Raynham for what should have been a relaxing vacation, she's been seeing *The Big Blue*.

Jessica is smelling things too—dead and rotting things that she can't see. She is sure those dead and rotting things are dead people. Lots of dead people.

Jessica's worst nightmares will soon become her reality. Her reality will soon become a terrifying nightmare.

The tentacled residents of the House of Death have a lot that they wish to show Jessica Schreiber. They have a lot that they wish to tell her. But will she survive long enough to learn their lessons?

Burning Bulb
PUBLISHING

WOL-VRIEY
BIZARRO AND TRANSGRESSIVE FICTION

BRAINCHEW

It was supposed to be a simple jewel heist, but it went badly wrong. Chuck got shot and died.

Lance hid his friend's corpse in the Pleasant Street Cemetery. But that was a big mistake—there was something undead, something extremely hungry . . . something eXXXtremely horrible, buried in the Pleasant Street Cemetery.

And Lance had just woken it up.

They called the monster Brainchew because it ate brains. Human brains. And it preferred those brains fresh from the heads . . . of the living.

And now it was awake again, Brainchew planned on feeding big-time tonight. Oh hell yes, it did.

BRAINCHEW 2: OUT OF THEIR HEADS

After Tiff Hooper recognizes Josh Penham, the man who abducted her and kept her in his basement and abused her, she brings her three friends to Raynham for a night of well-deserved revenge on him.

Only things don't go according to plan.

It is never a good idea to leave a corpse in Raynham's Pleasant Street Cemetery. You run the very real risk of awakening what lies underground there. And that thing—Brainchew—is more horrible and more evil than anything the average mind conceives of even in its worst nightmares.

Brainchew is back! And this time the monster is extra-hungry. But there are plenty of delicious human brains about tonight, and Brainchew intends to eat them all before dawn.

Burning Bulb
PUBLISHING

WOL-VRIEY
BIZARRO AND TRANSGRESSIVE FICTION

DARIA: AN EROTIC NIGHTMARE

Even the best laid women can go wrong.

Daria Simpson is HUNGRY. She's HUNGRY for sex and bloodshed and death.

Shelly Parker just wanted to have a threesome with her boyfriend Craig and her best friend Erica. Everything was shaping up nicely for their weekend of sexual fun and games, until they stopped at the creepy Crossway Diner and met Daria.

From the moment they met Daria, EVERYTHING went wrong for them; and it went wrong in the most horrific and terrifying of ways!

Daria: Paranormal service has been resumed.

WET BONES

Greg is about learning the hard way that you don't mess with Aunt Grace.

Nine completely fleshless skeletons recovered in the Massachusetts woods. Two detectives on the trail of a horrible, hungry monster.

Broken-hearted Allie Jackson has a date with a creature from Hell.

Things are about to get well out of hand for everyone, and in horrifying, terrifying ways they don't expect.

Burning Bulb

WOL-VRIEY
BIZARRO AND TRANSGRESSIVE FICTION

MR. UGLY

When a rotting corpse appears and starts butchering Raynham's youths, there's really only one question that needs answering:

Is this faceless and rotting monster Peter Howard, or isn't it?

Problem is, Peter Howard died 15 years ago. So how can he possibly be back from the dead and murdering people with such relentless and incredible brutality?

Peter's mother Malicia, who's just been released from the lunatic asylum may have the answers to the crazy puzzle, but the two detectives investigating the deaths don't even know the right questions to ask her yet.

BRUTAL

Jane Winters is 28 years old.

She works as a checkout cashier in a department store. She's an attractive woman with a winning personality. She has both a photographic memory and an I.Q. of 189.

She's met the man of her dreams.

But she's also a cannibal with a unique and very scary mode of operation.

The group known as TULIP (The Urban Legend Investigation People) are out to either prove or disprove the legend of Insane Jane.

But have TULIP bitten off more than they can chew?

Burning Bulb

WOL-VRIEY
BIZARRO AND TRANSGRESSIVE FICTION

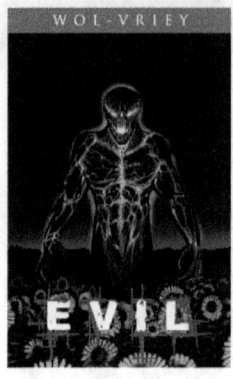

EVIL

The Evil began the week before Sylvia Stewart's 30th birthday.

Cathy Higgins died.

The Bargainer resurrected Cathy . . . for a price.

The price? Cathy's father Ronan had to plant some seeds for him.

But these were no ordinary seeds the Bargainer gave to Ronan Higgins. These were seeds from Hell: seeds which required human flesh as both soil and fertilizer.

And meanwhile, the unsuspecting Sylvia Stewart went ahead with the plans for her birthday party, which was to be held on Ronan Higgins' sunflower farm . . .

666

Ohio's State Route 666 stretches 14.7 miles between Zanesville and Dresden.

Most days, it's just a normal road with a funny name.

But for six minutes on the 6th of June each year, Route 666 becomes a gateway to somewhere else . . . a gateway to Hell.

Each year 13 unfortunates get trapped in the 666 underworld, with no way to get back home.

This year though, things are going to be very different. For one thing, there are currently a whole lot of turbulent human emotions at play in the underworld. And also . . . the psycho Al Gore is just about completing his collection of human heads.

And . . . what the hell is a church doing in Hell, of all places?

Burning Bulb
PUBLISHING

WOL-VRIEY
BIZARRO AND TRANSGRESSIVE FICTION

THE CLEAVERMAN

It began as a joke, a gag to pass the time that turned deadly. One rainy August night in Raynham, MA, nine friends jokingly invoke the evil phantom butcher called the Cleaverman.

These nine friends get a whole lot more than they ever bargained for. Because there's only one way to return the deadly Cleaverman back to the darkness he came from, and that is to solve his riddle, which starts: "Tell me the name of John Cleaverman's wife . . ."

And human beings being what we are, even with the Cleaverman out to butcher them all, our nine friends still manage to stir A WHOLE LOT of human misbehavior into the deadly mix.

At the rate they're going, it'll be a wonder if anyone survives THE CLEAVERMAN at all.

PERVERSE

When 21-year-old Heather Forrest accompanies three of her friends on a weekend trip up to Vermont, she has no idea what she's getting into.

Because, during a brief stop in the western Massachusetts woods, the girls get kidnapped and things go rapidly downhill from there. Soon Heather and her friends are fighting for their lives, fighting to survive the most perverted and impossible situation imaginable. And meanwhile, Hank Rollins is also in the woods, hunting the unholy monster that killed his wife and son . . . and he's hunting it with live human bait.

Oh yes, there will be blood. And there will be terror and buckets of gore also. And truly horrible atrocities will happen. Most definitely so.

Burning Bulb

WOL-VRIEY
BIZARRO AND TRANSGRESSIVE FICTION

THE VIRGIN

10 million dollars in prize money. 1000+ video cameras, lots of deadly weapons, 10 Suitors, 5 Virgins & 3 Hours . . . to keep your hymen intact.

Hailey Osborne wants to sell her virginity for a hundred thousand dollars. But then she's made an offer she really can't refuse: how about competing to win ten million dollars in a no-holds-barred underground game show, where all she has to do is remain a virgin?

There's just two problems:
1. Four other women also want that prize money.
2. There's ten suitors all contesting to take Hailey and the other virgins' precious hymens . . . by any means necessary . . .

But hey, it's just for 3 hours, right? How hard can it possibly be? Hailey Osborne is about to find out.

THE BOOK OF ATROCITIES

Bestselling author Drake Melville has been missing for three years now. Drake vanished after publishing The Bleeding Oysters, an epic novel that set new standards for depictions of sleaze and depravity and human monstrosity in popular fiction. On vanishing, however, Drake Melville left a message for everyone, saying he'd 'left town' to go work on his follow-up novel The Book of Atrocities. The problem was, no one could find Drake. It seemed like he'd vanished off the face of the Earth. And now, three years later, Drake has just sent messages to his ex-wife Liz, his current (and abandoned) wife Melody; and his younger sister Chloe . . . asking them to meet him in Raynham, MA. Drake says he's now completed The Book of Atrocities and is ready to present it to the world. But there's a whole lot that Liz, Melody, and Chloe Melville don't know about Drake's Book of Atrocities. And unfortunately they're on their way to find out those excruciatingly painful truths. Because, see, Drake Melville is a VERY EVIL man with a VERY EVIL plan . . .

Burning Bulb
PUBLISHING

WOL-VRIEY
BIZARRO AND TRANSGRESSIVE FICTION

THE FINAL GIRL

Here there be monsters . . . because we made them.

At a secret location, 8 young women assemble to compete on the ultimate reality/game show—The Final Girl. The 8 contestants are: A young wife and her grown-up stepdaughter, a police detective, a prostitute, a nurse, a school teacher, and unemployed twin sisters.

The Final Girl is a no-holds-barred show beamed to an audience on the Dark Web, a show where murder is permitted and mutilation is encouraged.

The Rules:
1. Avoid being killed and eaten by the show's monsters and bogeymen.
2. Find the prize money—24 million dollars in cash.
3. Hold on to the money.

But only 1 woman can win. And to win The Final Girl reality show, that woman will need to be even more bloodthirsty and ruthless than the show's monsters.

Have a seat, everyone. The most dangerous game is about to begin!

WOMEN

John Miller must die . . . TONIGHT!

Megan Kemp initially went to the Penderson Mansion to collect a debt. But from the moment she stepped in there, getting back outside proved extremely difficult. And then what had merely been difficult for Megan suddenly turned deadly. Because something was going on in the Penderson Mansion that night. Five VERY ANGRY women had a score to settle, and no obstacle on earth would stop them. . . . And no one would get in their way and live to tell the tale either.
"John Miller must die," the women had decreed, and it looked like the forces of Hell would help them accomplish their deadly aim tonight.

But as the night progressed, Megan, who was now trapped in a deadly game of cat and mouse in the Penderson Mansion, found that despite her own troubles, her biggest question was: "What the hell did John Miller do to anger these five women this much?"

Beware, folks . . . sometimes things really do go too far!

Burning Bulb

WOL-VRIEY
BIZARRO AND TRANSGRESSIVE FICTION

RATIO OF BROOKES TO ASHLEYS

After being cursed by a dying woman, Mike Broadman's love life completely nosedives. One girlfriend cheats on him and the next one dies a very messy death.

Next, a psychic informs Mike that he's under an evil spell that will keep killing his girlfriends, and that the ONLY solution (the ONLY way that he'll ever have a happy love life again) is for him to only date women named either Brooke or Ashley from now on.

Mike tries to comply with this, but still, the deaths continue, and now they're becoming even more brutal and bloody. Mike now finds himself in a race against time. He needs to 'equalize the ratio of Brookes to Ashleys' before it's too late.

And then, just when it seems things can't get any crazier or deadlier for Mike, he meets 'Brash' — the twins Brooke and Ashley Lawrence . . .

And the body count keeps rising . . .

DELICIOUS ZOMBIE

The zombie apocalypse happened two years ago. Today, zombies are mankind's new cattle. The undead are headed like cows and killed and eaten by everyone. The reason for this atrocity? Eating zombie meat has been scientifically proven to reverse human aging. Therefore, anyone who eats the zombies will live forever. Nowadays there are no old people anywhere on Earth. Everyone is young and healthy. Even deadly diseases have regressed. "

Digestion is Salvation," the Church of Zombie preaches. But three people—scientist Ethan Hackman, ex CIA assassin Paula Neyman, and socialite Zoe Patterson—seek to change this madness that is modern life.

With a group of ruthless and sadistic bounty hunters hot on their trail as they attempt to save the world, will Ethan, Paula, and Zoe succeed in curing the zombies, or will the age of the 'Delicious Zombie' continue? One thing is for certain, however; there will be a HUGE amount of murder and mutilation, bloodshed, violence and gore before the knotty issue of the zombies' food status is resolved.

WOL-VRIEY
BIZARRO AND TRANSGRESSIVE FICTION

MOTEL GOTHIC

The Devil's Coin Game was a game for desperate men. And Dooks, Hicks, and Robby were three such men, men with nothing to lose, men prepared to gamble their lives away on the flip of a coin. The rules of the game were simple: one man would die, the other two would have their wishes granted by the devil. At midnight in the Sunflower Motel, the Devil's Coin Game will be played, and one of the players will not survive.

Elsewhere in the Sunflower Motel, two female assassins Mandy Cherry and Dewdrop arrive to murder someone. But things are guaranteed to go awry when the intended victim is a witch.

And on this same portentous night, Roman is about to have an unforgettable meeting with a prostitute named Christine. Christine Valona supposedly brings bad luck to all those who encounter her; but why is this, and who is she?

THE BACHELOR

One eligible bachelor, thirteen gorgeous young women, and a TV crew, on a remote Pacific island paradise. What could possibly go wrong? A lot!

Tired of his refusal to get married and make her some grandchildren, American playboy Tyler Bradley is given a 90-day ultimatum by his wealthy mother to either get married or be disowned.

As a solution, Tyler's best friend, TV producer Disney Dizzford suggests that they hold a 'bachelor-seeking-love' themed reality show on Eternity Island, a remote island paradise off the coast of Guatemala, which for some reason the Guatemalan government pretends doesn't exist. "When the black cloud comes," the strange old man warned, "monsters will emerge from the sea. When the black cloud covers the sky, all will die."

But nobody takes the old guy seriously, because of course this is the 21st century and there are no such things as sea monsters, right? That sort of stuff only happens in bad movies, right?

Wrong. The black cloud just arrived over Eternity Island . . .

WOL-VRIEY
BIZARRO AND TRANSGRESSIVE FICTION

MARRIAGE

Adam Norwood, suffering from an extreme photosensitivity skin condition, resides on a secluded island with his wife, Phoebe, and his possible wizard of a father-in-law, Lester. Despite outward appearances of a happy marriage, Adam's life is plagued by recurring nightmares in which Phoebe repeatedly kills him, driving him to the brink of insanity. To add to his woes, Hilary Burton, an alluring party guest on Goat Island, mistakenly identifies Adam as her former lover and is determined to win him back, setting the stage for a calamity that threatens the lives of everyone on the island.

Adam's condition and nightmarish visions pale in comparison to the impending peril he's about to face. The arrival of Hilary Burton unravels a sinister chain of events that may jeopardize the very existence of the island's residents, pushing Adam to discover a new and dire meaning of "bad" and "deadly."

THE MAN WHO KILLED HIS WIFE

Maryanne Wilson's death was definitely an accident. Her husband Bob had absolutely no intention of killing her.

But it was almost certain that a court of law would see things differently, particularly after Bob had sex with Maryanne's corpse . . . and that was why Bob Wilson decided not to call in the police, but to seek an alternative solution to the problem he'd gotten himself into . . . A solution which unfortunately only made matters a whole lot worse for him.

Everything began because Bob Wilson was working too hard and as a result was neglecting his loving wife, Maryanne.

And so, Maryanne asked their upstairs neighbor Jennifer for help.

Jennifer Haskins apparently knew a little magic, and so she cast a spell on Bob, one that would help Maryanne get laid on a more regular basis, like every night if she so desired.

What could possibly go wrong with a simple arrangement like that? Everything you can't possibly imagine . . .